MOONWATER

Also by Claudette Nicole
The Mistress of Orion Hall
Bloodroots Manor
Circle of Secrets
The Haunting of Drumroe
The Dark Mill
The Haunted Heart
The Chinese Letter
Dark Whispers
When the Wind Cries

MOONWATER

CLAUDETTE NICOLE

CUTTING EDGE

ISBN-13: 978-1-957868-53-0

Published by
Cutting Edge Books
PO Box 8212
Calabasas, CA 91372
www.cuttingedgebooks.com

CHAPTER ONE

The night had taken over the world and the buttressed, swollen trunks of the cypresses swept upwards, rising from the still water, towering, primeval shapes, awesome sentinels of the blackness. The hanging roots of the mangroves, twisted fingers, dipped low and the girl stood alone in the dark, her small figure terribly fragile in the wispy nightgown, a spectral shape, an intruder, an interloper in this stygian kingdom of another world. And the dark water, licking at the mossy banks, beckoned silently. A half-moon, low in the sky, failed to pierce the dense, twisted tangle of aerial roots and foliage. The mimosa hung in the air, thick and cloying, as the girl's voice floated out into the darkness, soft, wavering.

"Pirie," she called. "Pirie, please come out." Her bare feet moved forward, hesitant on the marsh grass and the nut moss. The cinnamon fern brushed her legs as she paused, looking around her at the blackness, aimlessly searching.

"I saw you, Pirie," she called out again. "I saw you. Please don't hide anymore, Pirie. Please come out."

But only the soft hoot of an owl and the click-click of the cicadas answered the call and she moved slowly on, unmindful of the soft clutch of the spider web that brushed her forehead. And the dark water, licking the mossy banks, beckoned silently.

"Pirie," she called once more, her voice sing-song, strangely detached, a plaintive sound in the deep of the dark. "Pirie, Pirie, I. want to talk with you."

Nearly at the edge of the moss-covered bank now, she halted to raise her head and gaze upward into the gnarled, tangled vines and tendrils. Her eyes wide, staring, seemed to seek without knowing what they sought amid the leafy heritage of a dim and distant age. Trailing vines moved gently as the soft wind disturbed the hot, oppressive air and the slender, small figure stood still.

And the dark water, licking the mossy banks, beckoned silently.

Finally, as though it took great effort, the girl began to turn and retrace her steps through the darkness, moving slowly through the hanging curtain of leaves and trailing vines. The eyes of the night watched her go, silent eyes, waiting eyes, and as the girl emerged onto a lawn of soft grass, a whispered voice spoke in the dark.

"I told you so," the voice breathed bitterly. "Not until moonwater."

"We may not have time to wait," another voice answered in hushed tones.

The girl's slender figure passed through the soft embrace of a weeping willow hanging low with night dew. The leaves stretched out after the girl and then fell back, disappointed it seemed, and the creatures of the night resumed their activities in the dark world which was theirs.

And the dark water, licking the mossy banks, continued to beckon silently.

> *When you hear the whistle blow,*
> *You will know that I have gone,*
> *You will know that I have gone,*
> *Five hundred miles .....*

Pierette sang the words softly to herself and heard them blown back through the window of the speeding car. The guitar case rested in the rear seat and her fingers on the steering wheel formed the chords that accompanied the melody. It was automatic, a reflex action. How many times had she sung that song over the past two years? She could hardly guess and a small, almost derisive laugh escaped her. Pierette DuChamps, folk singer. And dreamer, slayer of dragons, conqueror of all that stood between herself and fame. Only it hadn't quite turned out that way. Not that it had gone badly. It just hadn't gone well, or not well enough. Singing and folk music, the basic, unvarnished language of the heart, had always been a part of her life, like breathing in and breathing out. At home, when her father and missy still lived, singing and guitar playing was a plain, everyday part of existence. There just wasn't a day that passed when someone didn't sing or strum a little. And when she'd left to conquer show business, she'd done so firmly steeped in the music she wanted to bring to the world. But there'd been no glamorous, unreal visions of instant success. Pierette had always been too level-headed for that. But she hadn't expected the grubbiness of it all, either; the auditions that were only excuses for something else. Lord, she recalled, how many of those had she stalked from before they came to realize she intended to make it on her singing, not her body. That would have been the easy road, Pierette knew. She had the tall grace, the high bust and long, slim legs which excited men. That excitement was fun to see, and she'd seen it flare in many men's eyes. It did great things for a girls ego but after a while it paled and lost a lot of its meaning. One came to look for other things, things harder to find. Pirie heard herself singing again. The song had stayed with her, filling her mind from the moment she'd closed the door to her little apartment and climbed into the battered old car which had brought her to the city in the first place.

> *You will know that I have gone,*
> *Five hundred miles .....*

They would know, all right, Pierette told herself with at least a soupçon of satisfaction. Her leaving would not go completely unmourned. Mr. Carmala, who owned the *Today Club* had tried to be understanding, in his own way, and she'd stayed at the small club longer than any of the other jobs she'd held. The boys in the trio, Benny and Butch and Raedich, who'd never been called anything else but Raedich, they would be sorry she had left. And of course Tony would have regrets, but only for a little while, she knew, realistically. He wasn't the type to hang onto regrets for very long. Flashing, dark-eyed Tony, only the latest in a succession of Tony's, different names and different faces but all filling the same role. She should have quit long ago, she knew, and yet she went on hoping to find a way to break through the sea of calculated commercialism that was called show-business today. But then the letter had come and now she was rushing back home, back to the bayou country, rushing amid a flood of fearful apprehensions. The letter lay inside her purse on the seat beside her, burning, demanding speculation. But she had forced herself not to think anymore than she had already about it. It was enough that it had sent a strange, shivery feeling through her when she'd read it. And of course, it had brought the past swirling into the present, threatening to engulf her in a whirlpool of old dislikes and unresolved feelings. There'd be all too much of that once she reached home, Pirie knew, and she'd have to face it all, each and every item that needed resolving. But it was the letter that had frightened her, that had given her the sudden, sharp, unexplained premonition of terrors yet to be faced. Pirie had never before felt, so strongly, those strange silent messages that transmit themselves in ways beyond our understanding.

Wrenching her mind from the cold fear and the letter, she watched the headlights probe the night like twin paintbrushes of light that made trees, curves, houses and fences magically appear upon a canvas of black. They painted an old barn, a huge oak tree and then a road sign and Pirie read the lone word: *Vicksburg.* A glow of diffused light appeared ahead and she knew it meant a roadside diner and she slowed the car. The straining old engine needed the stop even more than she did. She hadn't stopped since Turkeytown just off the Cumberland Plateau in Alabama and her mind flashed back to the procession of markers and road signs she'd left behind her: Saltville, Mountain City, Winchester, Shiloh, Union-town, Chickasaw Bluffs, all those "sharp names that never get fat," as Stephen Vincent Benét had written. Benét had always been her favorite poet and as a student at Greenbriar, *the* finishing school for young ladies, she had committed a good part of Benét to memory. One stanza, from *The Golden Corpse,* leaped into her mind and she just as quickly flung it away. Or tried to. The orange glow had become a square, garish neon sign on the left side of the road. A cluster of huge trailer trucks stood beneath its light, looking not unlike a herd of elephants at a water-hole. Pirie steered her little car into a small space between two silent mammoths. They were strangely comforting on the night roads, these huge trucks with their rows of bright lights twinkling behind them and at the front of their cabs. They helped to fend off the lonliness of the dark highways and, though beside them she felt fearfully small, they also comforted by their very size.

Pirie snapped off the ignition, turned on the roof light and looked at herself in the rear-view mirror. She saw light brown hair, not too wind-blown, and soft, hazel eyes, a little tired from driving. Her Breton blood had given her the dark eyebrows and thin, aquiline nose, while the English of her mother's side had bequeathed to her the creamy complexion. She straightened the aqua sweater and touched a hand to the large amulet that hung between her breasts. The smooth, opal stone was surrounded by nine small opals, each in its own lacy gold setting around the larger stone. She had never been terribly fond of the piece, nor of the woman who had given it to her on the day she left. But now, returning home, she had for some reason felt almost compelled to put it on. Valonia would be pleased to see her wearing it and at the thought of the woman, Pirie DuChamps' lips tightened involuntarily.

Taking her purse, she got out, locked the car and went into the harsh brightness of the diner. The truckers, big men with heavy arms, paused to appreciate her loveliness and made her momentarily feel less tired. She liked being admired and felt sorry for those women who were too afraid to admit enjoying it. That, too, was part of her French heritage: the open, honest enjoyment in being an attractive woman. She sat at the counter and ordered coffee, eggs and bacon from a peroxide blond waitress with empty eyes who, she knew, would be happy to see her leave.

She ate slowly and, without the road to occupy her attention, her mind kept returning to the letter inside her purse. Once again, she felt herself grow cold and frightened and she angrily turned her thought to Peely to let a warm glow of sisterly love and happy memories wrap themselves around her. Peely, laughing, eager, pixie-ish Peely, all tomboy and young lady mixed up together in one slim body. But, Pirie reminded herself, that was two years ago, when she'd left home after her mother's funeral. Two years ago! She turned the words over in shock. It seemed so much longer and yet it seemed only yesterday. She was twenty-three now and that would make Peely fifteen. Though there were eight years between them, she and her younger sister had always been very close, all through school and after. After for her, of course, because Peely was still a schoolgirl. Her mother, who let everyone call her Missy, always insisted on calling the girls by their baptised names, Pierette and Philine. Missy had that love for things of grace and beauty, the soft-edged things of life. But this was America, even in Louisiana bayou land with its heritage of old world French grace, and America only tolerates the echoes of other ways until she can put her own stamp of vitality and impatience on them. And so, Pierette and Philine quickly became Pirie and Peely, to most people anyway. In fact, Pirie recalled with a smile how happy she and her sister had been at the Americanization of their names, mostly a result of school-mates. After all, the ante-bellum days were gone; the romantic, courtly influences of the past were so much ancient history, liv-ing on only in the graciousness of individuals such as Missy. But she was older now, and with age had come understanding and an appreciation of both their names, and for the subtle meaning and influence that had come with them.

The waitress brought coffee and Pirie gazed into the dark liquid as she stirred it, watching the little whirlpools created by her spoon. Inside their concentric circles, like tiny frames, she saw the faces of yesterday come alive, her father, Missy, her friends at Grandview High School, Mrs. Callion at Greenbriar, Byron Lee Hodges and Peely's pixie countenance. She took a sip of the coffee and they all vanished; only the letter inside her purse remained. She finished the coffee quickly, letting the warmth trickle down to revive her spirits, paid the empty-eyed blond, and went out into the hot, thick night air. She carefully backed the little car from between the two huge trailer trucks and in moments she was hurtling through the darkness again, the road signs clicking off the history imbedded in this turbulent land. Feeling refreshed, she drove fast, feeling the need to hurry more for some unexplained reason. Perhaps because she was get-ting closer to home, Pirie told herself. Home. She grimaced. It even had a funny, unreal sound to it. She shivered, though the night wind was hot, and rolled the window up part way. She felt her hand fingering the smooth center stone of the nine-pointed amulet and, annoyed with herself, pressed down harder on the accelerator. The headlights, opening up the dark, outlined an old house, a silo, a broken fence, the amber glow of a cat's eyes along-side the road, a curve coming up, and then, with frightening sud-denness, it happened. Another car came around the curve, its lights no brighter than a thousand others she'd passed that night, and at the same instant her eyes picked out the highway marker with the huge number 9 marking the route. Then suddenly the interior of her car was ablaze with sudden shafts of light that flew onto the windshield and back into her eyes, blinding, dazzling shafts that flung themselves about with lightning-like speed. The girl felt the twist of her hands turning the wheel into the path of the oncoming car, almost as if other hands were pulling the wheel away from her. She screamed as she heard the sound of the other car's tires and she wrenched the wheel back, turning it in the opposite direction. The car hit the depressed shoulder of the road and she clung to the wheel, fighting to hold it steady as she was slammed against the door. The handle was a sharp, stabbing pain in her side and she heard stone and gravel being thrown up by the wheels. She pressed on the brake and felt the tortured strain of metal as the car finally came to a shuddering halt and there was only the rising cloud of dust and the wild beating of her heart.

The girl sat there, gathering herself, grateful that she could say she was alive. She reached back and touched the guitar, grateful for its reassuring feel. Still shaking, the blood pounding in her temples, she tried the door handle and found it worked. As she crawled out she put a hand under her sweater to explore the sharp, stabbing pain in her side. There was no blood but she knew she'd carry the bruise for a long time. She walked slowly around the car, through the beam of the headlights that penetrated the night. The right side of the car bore a new collection of dents and scrapes where she'd sideswiped the trees and road reflector posts. Other than that, there was no serious damage and, her knees still watery, she sat back in the car and tried to recollect what had happened. The other car had gone on its way and all she could recall was the strange and frightening incongruity of it all. There'd been the headlights and the big roadsign number 9 and then the blinding eruption of dazzling shafts of light. Her fingers touched the amulet at her chest and she frowned. Had the other car's headlights struck the stones of the amulet and caused the blinding shafts of light to leap up and strike her eyes? It was a possible explanation but her thoughts had to linger on something more frightening: she thought of how her hands had turned the wheel *into* the path of the other car. Why, she asked herself, starting to tremble as she thought about it. She had heard of those unexplainable moments when death pulls at the living. Most people have experienced a touch of it in one way or another, often standing at the edge of a high place. But this was no touch of it. This was a force twisting her hands, unmistakably twisting them. Her skin was suddenly cold and damp with beads of perspiration as she pulled the car door closed.

Whatever had caused it, whatever strange forces had conspired, she had managed to cheat death of a victim and her determined character asserted itself at once. She snapped on the ignition and heard the engine come to life and the little car, began to pull itself out of the depression at the side of the road. Her lips grim, Pirie drove on. Whatever tiredness had been in her, it was now driven away and she decided to keep going, keeping her speed down to reasonable limits. She lifted the amulet from around her neck with one hand and put it on the seat. Her watch told her she could be home by dawn if she could keep driving. Her pretty face set, determined, she knew she'd be there by dawn.

CHAPTER TWO

When Pirie turned from the highway onto the macadam road, the neat road sign bore the lone word GRANDVIEW and the gray light of day moved slowly across the land. Almost instantly, she was in Bayou country with the huge willows hanging low to narrow the road. On both sides of her she saw the familiar swamps with their canals and estuaries of slow-moving waters, the vast beds of hyacinths and the bal cypresses rising out of the water like creatures from some forgotten age. Here and there she spotted the pure-white petals and red stamen of the swamp lily, brilliant against the vast acres of pickerel weed. But there'd be time for exploring old haunts, for renewing old friendships with things growing and green. Right now she wanted to get home, and at the word "home" she again reacted, this time with a silent, wry smile. She wasn't really going home and she ought to stop referring to it that way, she told herself sternly. She was going back to a place where she'd been raised, where she'd known happiness and love, a place that had once been home. But it no longer was that. When had it ceased to be home? The wry smile crossed her face again. That was hard to answer with pinpoint accuracy but it started sometime around the time Robert Barlow began courting her mother.

It hadn't been loyalty to her father. Heavens, he'd passed away too long ago for that and once she had even asked herself, candidly, if she were jealous of Missy's new happiness. And, candidly, she had searched her soul and discarded the thought. After her father had died there had been just she, Peely and

Missy in the big house, except for the servants, of course, and she knew it would be good for her mother to remarry. She had wanted that for her. So it hadn't been old loyalties but the man himself, Robert Barlow. Psychologists might have classified it as a personality conflict, but there had never been any open conflict between her and Barlow. And undeniably, he had made Missy happy. Originally European, he spoke English impeccably with the merest trace of a charming accent. But Pirie had never liked him, never felt anything but suspicion and distrust for the man and she had no reasons to explain her feelings. And then he had brought the woman, Valonia, in as housekeeper and lightened the chores for everyone. Valonia, gaunt-faced, efficient, with deep, burning eyes that seemed to have been borrowed from some eagle long departed, had taken command of the house at once. She had always been polite and concerned over Peely and herself, Pirie knew, but she could never bring herself to like the woman. She could never shake the strange thought that Robert Barlow and the woman had some bond, some secret bond that went far beyond an employer-employee relationship. That was a silly, unfair thing to think, too, she had often told herself, and maybe it stayed in her only because he had brought the woman in from someplace distant which was never clearly explained. But when Missy suddenly grew ill, and death came with unexpected speed, she and Robert Barlow had only been married two years. When that time came, with Peely completing her last year at Grandview High and enrolled in Greenbriar where she would board, Pirie saw no reason to stay any longer at the house. She had left to carve out a career for herself, Robert Barlow's promise to look after Peely ringing in her ears, Valonia's promise to look after the house a subtle counterpoint. The house, she knew then, was a matter for discussion at some future date. At that time, she was happy to have Barlow stay on there with Valonia to keep after the place. Her father had left it to Peely, knowing Pirie hadn't really wanted it, hadn't ever liked it that much. But he'd made Pirie trustee for her younger sister until the girl reached eighteen.

A purple gallinule startled her as it took wing in a burst of color and she saw that warm shafts of sun, striking through the willows in the early morning heat, were sending the night mists up from the water to evaporate. The marsh wrens were starting their morning chatter and the road turned from its path through the bayou land to move over flat country and widened unexpectedly into the main street of Grandview. The high school greeted her as she entered town, red brick with white cupolas at each end and the sight of it flooded the girl's mind with a hundred separate memories. The town itself still slept as she drove down Main Street. Letting her mind fill up with its memories, she saw all the old, familiar places come alive again. Her eyes took in the bright yellow sign of Rumson's Ice Cream Parlor, the Post Office, the small gas station at the corner of Catalpa and Main, Sheriff Whittaker's office, LeClerq's Variety store and Madame Duval's Dress Shoppe where she'd gotten her graduation gown. The short block of two story offices still nudged the lumber yard and she suddenly felt a surge of gladness for those things that stay the same, that give life a kind of reassurance. It didn't take long to pass through Grandview. There wasn't that much of it and soon she was beyond the town and the bayou country took over again. The macadam road ended and became a dirt spur; she was now deep in bayou land where the morning mists still hung as a white blanket over the water, the great cypresses were as ghostly giants. Hanging mangroves and willows scraped the roof of the car. Searching the trees rising out of the canals at the edge of the moss-covered bank, her eyes found the one she sought, the one with the two big, scarred "knees," the conical shapes that protruded from the water around the base of the Cypress. She almost exclaimed aloud as she found it because it meant she was on DuChamps land now and as the road made a sharp turn, the great house stood before her, appearing almost magically through the low, lance-shaped leaves of a big willow. The sign in the ground bore the one word in weathered gold paint on a white background:

Moonwater.

The house towered upwards, reaching into the hanging vines and Pirie forced herself to gaze at its baleful sinisterness as it sat there like some gigantic toad, the two round windows over the front entrance its unblinking eyes, and the stone, castle-like turrets on both ends its legs. It had always been, in her father's words, "beautifully ugly," but while he and Missy were there she could live with its ugliness, even laugh at it. When Robert Barlow came, and then the housekeeper Valonia, the huge place had grown more and more frightening until it was no longer even "beautifully ugly" but evil, threatening, malevolent. It was then that she learned that the character of houses, like that of people, stems from what takes place within them. She saw herself again, on so many nights before she decided to leave, lying fearfully in her room, sheets pulled tight to her face, as the trailing vines slithered across the roof and the house seemed alive with what Stephen Vincent Benét called the "small, dim noises, thousand-fold, that all old houses and forests hold."

The twin white columns of the entranceway had gathered a new layer of clinging vines, she noted, and the Willows, Acacia, Blackgum and Sassafras still framed the place with only the road, curving on past the right, opening a pathway through their denseness.

Moonwater, Pirie uttered the name silently, named for those few nights every month when the full moon broke through the curtain of the trees to shine upon the bayou just behind the house and turn the slow-moving water into a ghostly silver-blue ribbon. On those nights, the bayou came alive as it did at no other time, as the moonwater beckoned the creatures of the night. Moonwater,

Pirie repeated, a house whose history had been lost in the mists of antiquity and whose name alone survived. Her father had bought it from the estate of an old recluse. The only records that existed in the Louisiana parish had been destroyed when the old courthouse had burned over a hundred years before. Only the name had survived. As she stood before the massive house her thoughts were cut off by the opening of the heavy, oak door and the tall, gaunt-faced woman who came out. A long, dark gray dress clothed her heavy-boned body and she wore her hair pulled back severely.

"Pierette," she called out. "What a wonderful surprise. I heard a noise as I got up, looked out my window and saw you getting out of your car."

"Hello, Valonia," the girl answered, trying to put some warmth into her voice and knowing it was an unsuccessful try. Valonia was one of those people who, smiling, managed to look severe.

"We weren't sure you were coming, my dear," the woman said, her voice deep, and Pirie caught the meaning of her words at once. They were aware that Peely had written but only that she had written. The contents of the letter were unknown to the woman, at least, or she'd have no need to wonder whether the girl would come. Valonia was reaching into the back seat of the car, unloading suitcases, using her left hand for the heaviest ones and Pirie realized she'd almost forgotten the woman was left-handed.

"Peely's note decided me to come back for a visit," Pirie said. "She said she hasn't returned to Greenbriar since spring vacation." She hoped desperately that she sounded no more than casually concerned. The woman's hard, burning eyes told her nothing. Pirie took her guitar case in one hand and followed Valonia to the house.

"Peely's not been well," the woman said. "We didn't write you because we didn't want to worry you. Mr. Barlow said that carving a career in the entertainment field was enough of a job without adding worries to it."

Pirie permitted herself a small smile of appreciation.

"Your room is all ready for you and just the way you left it," the woman went on. As they reached the big, heavy door of the house it swung wide and Robert Barlow stood there in trousers and deep red smoking jacket, his rich voice booming out a welcome. He was still a handsome man, Pirie noted at once, with that patrician face and silver hair. His face was one that was just a little too much of everything, she'd always thought: a little too handsome, a little too fine, a little too weak. But that had been a minority opinion, she knew.

"What a great way to start the day," Robert Barlow boomed and his arm embraced her. Pirie held herself still, fighting down the impulse to tear away. "Peely's still asleep but as soon as she wakes we'll tell her you're here. I suspect you want to go to your room to freshen up a bit before breakfast."

Pirie nodded, grateful for the chance to move out from under his arm. Valonia was at the top of the stairs already and the girl hurried after her.

"We'll talk about Peely, later," the woman said as she opened the door to Pirie's room and the ominous hint in her voice made the knot in the girl's stomach grow tighter. But her room reached out to embrace her like an old friend and she closed the door behind her. Everything was indeed the way she'd left it, the old Bible atop her dresser, the three blue jeans hanging in the closet, the stuffed animal Byron Lee Hodges had given her still on the chair. She was unpacking when she heard the sound of footsteps in the hall and a peremptory knock. The door opened before she could get to it and Valonia was there, the opal amulet in her hand.

"It was on the car seat," she said, her eyes hard, piercing.

"I had it on," Pirie said, feeling unaccountably defensive. "I took it off this morning. It felt so heavy suddenly." The woman grunted and laid the nine-pointed amulet on the dresser and left, wordlessly. Pirie wondered why she had kept silent about her near-fatal accident. Was it merely her dislike of the woman that had kept her quiet? She shook off that thought, something unrealized refusing it. Somehow, unreasonable as it seemed, she had the strangest feeling that the woman would have derived some satisfaction from knowing. It was a vicious thought for Pirie and she felt ashamed for having had it. Or almost ashamed.

In the bathroom, she let soap and cool water wash the dust and grime from her body. Then she changed into slacks and a bright, orange blouse. She went to her purse and took out the letter and, seated on the bed, re-read it again, though each word was almost imprinted in her mind by now.

Dearest Pirie:

It is hot here but I am cold. I haven't been feeling well and stayed on here after spring vacation. I think you ought to come back or stay away but make up your mind. This sneaking in and out by night really ought to stop. Why do you do that? Please come in and talk to me next time. I feel so tired, so awfully tired.

Love, Peely.

Once again she wondered what it meant, what the strangeness of it said. She hadn't been near Moonwater for two long years and here was Peely writing about her sneaking in and out by night. But she had returned to get the answer and she wouldn't rest until she did. Suddenly she heard the sounds of running footsteps in the hall and then the door was flung open.

"*Pirie!*" the girl cried and rushed into her arms, burying her head in her shoulder and Pirie was grateful for that embrace for she could not have kept the shock out of her eyes. It was Peely, all right, but not the Peely she knew. This was a wan, hollow-cheeked, opaque-eyed girl, not the gay, sparkling, vivacious youngster she had always known. Pirie pushed back from her younger sister's embrace and let her eyes search the girl's face and linger on the wide, almost staring eyes. She felt Peely's body through the nightgown, trembling slightly. Her arms were full and soft. It was her face that reflected a lost, inner aimlessness.

"I got your note and decided you needed some cheering up," Pirie exclaimed, infusing her voice with false gaiety. Peely's burst of energetic excitement at seeing her seemed to have evaporated and the younger girl eased herself down on the bed slowly.

"What's wrong, hon?" Pirie asked. "Haven't you been feeling well?" It was an inane question but she felt she had to start someplace and she watched closely as Peely answered.

"I guess I feel all right," she said. "Sometimes, that is. I don't really know what's wrong, Pirie. I can't concentrate. I'm always so terribly tired. I see strange things and I feel like I'm going to die."

She spoke without emotion, with complete matter-of-fact simplicity and her words were all the more chilling because of it.

"What makes you say something like that, Peely?" she asked the younger girl and saw the vacant, empty stare in Peely's eyes. When her sister didn't answer, Pirie shook her gently by the shoulder.

"What makes you feel like you are going to die, Peely?" she asked.

"I don't know, Pirie," the girl answered. "I only know I get to feeling all cold sometimes and I kind of float through space and I just feel that way, that's all."

"That's a ridiculous way to feel," Pirie said, keeping her voice light while her heart grew tight in fear. Peely looked up at her with her eyes wide, staring, and then an expression crept into them.

"It is ridiculous, isn't it?" the younger girl answered, brightening for a moment and flashing a smile. "Maybe it'll all go away now that you're here. Oh, Pirie, it's so good to see you. Tell me all about life in show biz."

Pirie began to talk as she unpacked her things, using the opportunity to study and watch Peely. She told her of the good things that had happened, the funny things, the warm things and left out all that was ugly and cheap, while, as she talked, she continued to cast penetrating glances at her sister. Peely would listen for moments, and for brief flashes become her old, animated self. Then she would stare vacantly into space, hearing but not listening, there but really somewhere else. When Pirie finished unpacking she and Peely went downstairs to breakfast. Robert Barlow joined them and once again Pirie saw that Peely's attention was limited to brief spurts. Mid-way through breakfast, which was served in the spacious old kitchen on the long, wooden table, Peely pushed her plate of pancakes and sausages away and got up. She had come to breakfast wearing only her nightgown and Pirie had said nothing, waiting to see if her sister would pause to put on a dressing gown. When she hadn't, they had gone down and Pirie had mentally noted how unlike Peely that was.

"I'm tired," Peely announced, a sullenness in her tone. "I'm going to my room." She looked at Pirie for a long moment, as though trying to focus in on her properly and finally broke into a smile. "We'll talk some more later," she said. "All right, Pirie?"

"Of course, hon," Pirie answered, forcing a smile again that disappeared the moment Peely's back was turned and she watched the girl slowly mount the wide steps in the main hallway. Peely's room was also on the second floor but at the far end of the other wing of the house. When she was sure that her sister was safely out of earshot, Pirie turned to Robert Barlow and Valonia, who was quietly clearing away the dishes. She was sorry for the savagery of her tone but she couldn't keep it hidden.

"What in God's name has been going on here?" she shot out. "Peely's sick, terribly sick. Why didn't you notify me at once?"

Robert Barlow answered quickly, as if to prevent Valonia from speaking.

"Yes, my dear, Peely is ill," he agreed. "She seems to be having some mental or emotional problems, frankly. We've been terribly concerned about her, of course. Especially since it all came on so suddenly and with no apparent reason."

His tone, placating, soothing, only irritated Pirie more. His handsome face seemed so completely in control of things, so above it all.

"As for writing you, my dear," he went on, "Valonia's already touched on that."

Pirie, her mind crackling, wondered how he knew that. Only she and Valonia had been there when that came up. Had the woman told him of their brief conversation already? Or was that a convenient excuse they'd agreed to use long ago?

"Yes, I know," Pirie said, not caring about the sarcasm that coated her words. "You didn't want me to worry while I was carving my name in lights on Broadway." She was going to add a short, coarse expletive. Two years in show business had taught her the value of coarseness at times. But she held back and listened to Robert Barlow's smooth, resonant voice drone on.

"In addition, we've been right on top of the situation," he said. "That's why we kept her from returning to Green-briar, so she could be here, under constant care and supervision. She's been under a doctor's care but both diagnosis and treatment in this kind of thing is very difficult."

"Sometimes she sees things," Valonia's voice chimed in. "And of course, the mentally disturbed are in touch with elements we can but imagine."

The use of the term "mentally disturbed" infuriated Pirie.

"There must be some reason for this all of a sudden," she snapped back. "One doesn't become 'mentally disturbed,' to use your words, overnight. Peely's only been at Greenbriar for one year, now. Till she went away, she was living here and finishing at Grandview. Did you notice anything strange about her actions then?"

Robert Barlow shook his head, concern in his face. Pirie had tossed out the question to get a reaction more than anything else. There'd been nothing wrong with Peely during the last two years, when she first had gone away. Pirie would bet her life on that. Peely had written regularly and often, and her letters had been full of her usual, vivacious self. This girl that she had seen today couldn't have written those letters. She gazed at Robert Barlow and his look of sincere concern made her feel slightly ashamed at her own hostility.

"We don't think you should become unduly alarmed," he said. "Doc Asher feels that this could be only a temporary condition, perhaps brought on by some inner conflict connected with her maturing."

"*Doc Asher?*" Pirie almost screamed the name. "Doc Asher? That ... that *quack?* You ... you're having him treat Peely?" She groped for words and found them tumbling about inside her too fast to use. Doc Asher had been practicing in the back country for years, treating patients with a combination of ancient techniques, medicine man quackery and primitive methods. Her father, she recalled, said he wouldn't let the man "cut a hangnail."

"Doc Asher is a perfectly good doctor," Robert Barlow was saying. "He's one of a fast-disappearing, unappreciated breed, the true country doctor."

"The true country doctor my ass," Pirie exploded. "He's an old fraud, a medicine man." She saw the coldness in Robert Barlow's smile, the cold anger of his eyes. Valonia's face was set in ice. "What happened to Doctor Gallagher?" Pirie demanded, her blood boiling in anger.

"We felt Doc Asher was better for this problem," Robert Barlow said evenly. "Doctor Gallagher is away at least two to three times a week, operating at the new hospital in Cotile. When he's at Grandview, his in-town practice keeps him very busy. We felt that Doc Asher would be more able to give Peely the kind of attention she needed and so far we've been right. He's come whenever we've called him."

Logical, reasoned explanations. Why did she feel they meant nothing? "I want Peely examined by Doctor Gallagher," she said, flatly.

"That would be highly improper," Robert Barlow answered. "I suggest you have a talk with Doc Asher, first. He may surprise you and you may learn a few things."

Pirie looked up at Valonia's stern face as she stood behind Robert Barlow's chair, a face carved of stone, as if her very presence were supplying a grim strength to the man. Pirie held back the words that danced at the tip of her tongue. Only a few moments ago she had felt almost guilty at their apparent concern but now she sensed the very firm resistance to bringing in Doctor Gallagher. Was it only the resistance of those whose judgement has been questioned, she wondered? Or was it something else? There was something terribly wrong here at Moonwater, the girl sensed, and Peely's sickness was only a part of it. It was hanging in the very air, unseen, yet nonetheless there. She didn't want to be guilty of overdramatizing and what she felt was not made up of logic or reason or rational explanation. She knew, by some inner warning, that she had to be careful and clever as well as determined. But emotionalism would only complicate matters, she knew. She had to apply reason to what seemed beyond reason, to find the practical explanation for that which seemed beyond explaining. Her mind flashed back to that moment only a few short hours earlier when the lights had blinded her and her hands had twisted the wheel into oncoming death. It was only the fright and confusion of the blinding shafts of light, no doubt reflected from the nine-pointed opal amulet. She had simply twisted the wheel the wrong way in error and then caught herself. She pushed down a rush of questions that fought to be heard inside her mind. She would have none of them, she told herself angrily. Not yet, anyway.

"What treatment has Doc Asher been prescribing for Peely?" she asked, trying to sound casual. "I presume he has her on something."

"Of course," Valonia replied, quickly. "But you know the way doctors write and that medical code they use. I can't make anything out of it. Besides, he's given Peely a number of injections of something or other for her nerves."

Pirie smiled. Another reasonable reply that said nothing and revealed less.

"Does he still grind most of his own prescriptions?" she questioned sweetly. Robert Barlow fielded that one, a small smile of tolerance perched on his finely molded lips, infuriating in its condescension.

"I believe he does," the man answered smoothly. "And that's one of the reasons we like him so much. He takes time and trouble for his patients. He's not one of those pill pushers."

Pirie held her tongue again and returned Robert Barlow's smile with one of her own—sweet, gracious and twice as insincere.

"Is the buckboard still in the barn, and are the horses still there in condition?" she asked, abruptly switching the subject.

"Of course," Robert Barlow replied. "You need a buckboard to get through the back country roads. Or use one of the boats. But you know that, Pierette."

"Well, maybe I'll go pay your Doc Asher a visit at that," the girl answered. "But I'll call him for an appointment, first. However, Doctor Gallagher is going to examine Peely, too. I can assure you of that."

She walked from the kitchen, letting the last sentence lay there, not waiting for an answer or a comment. She walked through the wide center hall with its dark oak wood paneling and the heavy bannister that led to the second floor. The nearly black wood of the heavy hall chairs, black maple grown darker with the passage of time, added to the somber, depressing air of the main foyer and the girl hurried out into the sunlight. She walked to the side of the house and crossed under the large willow to the barn and the stables. Old Baldy, a big black gelding with a white blaze over his forehead, whinnied as she entered the stable. As she stroked the horse's head she heard footsteps behind her and turned to see Thomas the stableman, a friendly face from out of the past. She was frankly surprised that Barlow had continued to maintain the house in the same style. Of course, the income for Moonwater and the land came from the proceeds of rental properties her father had developed as far north as the Arkansas border. Though the house itself was Peely's, Barlow had the income from the properties as part of his inheritence at Missy's death. She exchanged small talk with old Thomas and then went back into the sunlight. Almost automatically, her footsteps led her to the garden alongside the east wing of the house. Missy had made the garden one of her favorite spots and, though the stone path still wound through the hibiscus and the spider lilies, the place had seen better days. A small furrow broke Pirie's smooth forehead as she approached a sizeable bed of not unattractive plants lining the wall of the house. Almost two feet tall, they bore a single stem which branched off into two leaf stems, each with a large leaf almost nine or ten inches across. Where the two leaf stems joined the main stalk, a single creamy white flower with golden stamens grew. As she bent over to peer more closely at the plants, she felt the presence of another person and she looked up to see Valonia standing by the side door of the house.

"They're new in the garden," Pirie said. "Did you plant them? What are they?"

"Mandrake," Valonia said. "They just came up by themselves."

"Mandrake?" the girl repeated, trying to recollect what, if anything, the name meant to her and quickly deciding it meant nothing. But then, there were many kinds of plants and flowers she knew little about. When she said nothing further, Valonia turned and went back into the house. Pirie walked to the front door, went up to Peely's room and looked in on the younger girl. Peely was sleeping soundly, her eyes dark and hollowed, her blond hair a cascade of gold on the pillow. Pirie left a note she quickly scrawled on a notepad by the bedside and softly closed the door behind her. It told her sister that she was going into town and would be back in the afternoon.

Pirie got into the car and drove off, casting a glance back at the house, hoping it might look less malevolent, but knowing it wouldn't.

CHAPTER THREE

A s she drove toward town, Pirie realized that she was operating on nervous energy—and that she would suddenly be
caught up in complete and utter exhaustion before the day was
out. The long, grueling drive, the tensions inside her, the sleep-
less night—they would all descend upon her in one, sudden rush.
Until they did, she would use every moment to try and approach
this strange and awesome problem with logic and reason, sepa-
rating fact from fancy. But even as she said that she smiled wryly
to herself. It would be hard enough anywhere, but here, in this
superstition-steeped country, in this land never freed from
ancient beliefs, it might be well-nigh impossible.

She drove along the bayou road and thought about this land
and its mist-shrouded waters, its hanging cypresses and closed-
in atmosphere. The people were but reflections of the nature of
the land itself, and even those who had broken with the spell of
the bayous, such as those in town, were not entirely removed
from its powers.

And so Pirie let her mind sort out what facts she knew,
assigning to each item a niche of its own. The first fact was that
Peely was ill, terribly ill in some strange, awesome way. The second fact was that she would find out what was wrong and do so
as quickly as possible. Or was that really a fact, she had to ask
herself. No, it was a determination and nothing more and she
saw that facts were something she didn't have, except the one of
Peely's illness. All the rest of what she had became quickly lost in
a welter of hazy, undefined emotions and underlying attitudes.

She knew she had to try to contain her own biases, but she had to wonder why Barlow and Valonia had shown such resistance to having Peely examined by Doctor Gallagher? It was almost as if they were in some way connected to Peely's illness, and perhaps felt responsible for it. Yet she had nothing to substantiate such a thought, Pirie knew. Once again, she would have to stop letting her long dislike of the couple and the sinister atmosphere of Moonwater color her thinking, she told herself reproachfully.

The nose of the old car was pushing it's way into Grandview and now the town's streets were alive with cars and pick-up trucks, people ambling along the narrow sidewalks, back country farmers and pickers gathered in small clusters for a moment of talk. The women, for the most part, wore simple, neat mail-order-catalogue dresses and the men were mostly shirt-sleeved and in work pants. She had forgotten how lean and sparse these people were and the soft, slurred drawl of the Louisiana speech, interspersed with the patois of the cajun dialect, formed a musical background as she drove slowly, looking for a spot to park. She found one almost directly in front of the brick and frame building that served Doctor Gallagher as office, residence and sometimes emergency hospital. But Doctor Gallagher, it turned out, was in Cotile for the day and would only be back tomorrow, according to a young woman in a nurse's uniform. Doctor Gallagher, a confirmed bachelor, had always picked out attractive young women as his assistants. Pirie, annoyed at herself for not having checked by phone, left her name and said she'd call in the morning.

As she was in town, she decided on a walk down Main Street. It became a succession of pauses and extended stops as she met a steady procession of old friends and acquaintances. People and places she'd consigned to memory's scrap-book as a past part of her life were suddenly very much alive again. A world she'd left, more or less for good, she had thought, had once more reached out to embrace her. But she was seeing these old schoolmates, friends, townsfolk and neighbors with different eyes, and it was a strange sensation, as though she were standing outside as well as inside a window and viewing things from both sides. She saw warmth and simple goodness but also inward provincialism. She saw welcome but also wariness. She saw admiration and envy and, as she talked with her many old friends, most now settled down to life in the bayou country, she realized that society in Grandview was just as stratified as in New York, Chicago or Los Angeles. In fact, she mused, Grandview was essentially a microcosm of the larger urban centers with, if anything, more rigidity in its social composition. But it was fun, nonetheless, being greeted with exclamations of delight. The local paper had, she knew, run a few pieces on her career and she had made one national TV appearance as part of a folk music festival and she basked in that aura of awe surrounding the local girl who had made a name, albeit a small one, in the glamorous field of show business. If they only knew, Pirie murmured inwardly to herself.

She had just walked out of LeClerq's Variety store when a voice called her name and she halted at once. It was a voice she'd heard almost every day and evening for nearly two years, a voice which most people thought she'd be hearing as a husband's call. A flood of memories rose up to wash over her as she turned to see the young man leaning out of the baby-blue convertible, boyishly good-looking with black, unruly hair.

"Well, I'll be damned," he was saying. "I thought I was seeing things."

Pirie's smile was wide and her hazel eyes sparkled almost impishly. "You're not seeing things, Byron Lee Hodges," she said. "It's really me, back in Grandview."

The man vaulted over the door of the car without opening it and stood before her, his eyes frank in their excitement as he took in the long, slender line of her figure, the softly-rounded hips and long legs. Standing before Byron Lee Hodges, she saw he had the same reckless good looks and she wondered why she had turned away from him. Was it only the desire for a career that had so burned inside her? No, she knew, there had to be more, but whatever it was she had pushed it so deep into the recesses of her mind that she could no longer summon it at once. Byron Lee was the last of one of the oldest families in Louisiana, a social "catch" almost any girl would have been eager to achieve. True, the Hodges lived more on pretensions of the past than on substance and she recalled her father saying that they constantly "treaded that fine line between gentility and solvency." Still, with his dashing, dark handsomeness, a proud, aristocratic kind of good looks, Byron Lee Hodges was a much-sought-after young man.

"You're looking wonderful, Byron Lee," Pirie said. "Still a bachelor?"

"Still a bachelor," he said. "I haven't succumbed yet. In fact, I've been wanting to see you so much that I was about to try to find out how to reach you by letter, and here you turn up in Grandview."

"You mean you're still thinking about me?" Pirie laughed. "What's happened to all the beautiful girls of the bayou country?"

"Oh, they're around but you're not the kind one forgets," he said, his smile meaningful.

"No hard feelings or bad memories?" Pirie laughed. "Let's be honest, Byron. When I left we weren't exactly speaking to each other."

"That's all old and past," he smiled. "I'm not the same kid and you're not the same girl. I'd like to start over. How about dinner tonight?"

He must have noted the moment of hesitation for Pirie saw a fleeting frown cross his face. She wanted especially to spend this first night back at Moonwater with Peely. There was so much more to watch and observe and learn.

"Tonight is no good for me, Byron," she said.

"Tomorrow night, then," he said, quickly. "Now that you're here, time's a-waisting."

She frowned inwardly at the remark. It seemed to say more than it did. But she saw no harm in a dinner out and it would be fun renewing old acquaintances with Byron. He was always insistent, almost arrogantly so, and this quality seemed to have increased. His very waiting for her answer had an impatient arrogance to it that used to irritate her. Now it was more amusing than anything else.

"All right," she laughed. "Tomorrow night."

"I'll be there at seven," he said and, with typical southern, Louisiana gallantry, bowed low. Always a Hodges, Pirie thought to herself as she watched the car roar off and his arm wave back at her. A girl would have to be made of stone not to react to his handsome, devil-may-care good looks and she was far from stone. There was a physical, animal sensuousness about Byron Lee Hodges that was inescapably exciting. She would enjoy going out with him again, she knew, and yet a small, murmuring voice inside her wished she could recall what it was that finally decided her to turn away from him three years before. She was walking back to her car when she heard her name called again, this time by a rich, calm voice, a voice with warmth and a hint of laughter in it.

"Pierette DuChamps," it said. "Welcome back."

Pirie turned to see the man, brown hair cut short with a tint of red in it and sparkling blue eyes in an amiable face, more beguiling than handsome. He wore an air of calm, self-assured strength the way most people wear their skin. She knew the face and then, as she searched her memory, she cried out.

"Adam Bailey!" she exploded.

"I was wondering how long it would take you," he said, his smile impish, teasing.

"Forgive me," she apologized, feeling herself redden. "It's just that I've met so many old faces and friends this morning."

"And we really only brushed past each other when we were in school," he added, and she was taken by the gracious way he instantly relieved her of any embarrassment. And he was right, of course. Adam Bailey had been two classes ahead of her and they'd traveled in different crowds.

"If I remember, you went away to college as soon as you graduated," Pirie said. "While I was still a struggling student."

"That's right," Adam Bailey said. "To a college in the midwest where I worked as hard as I could." He smiled at her and examined her beauty, she saw, with a frankness that was both honest and appreciative. There was a quiet, rugged strength about him that was strangely comforting.

"And now?" Pirie questioned.

"Adam Bailey, attorney-at-law, at your service," he grinned. "Ten Main Street."

"I'm impressed," Pirie said. "Though I didn't think there was enough to occupy a bright, eager young attorney here in the Bayou country."

"Well, I get around," he laughed. "I've an office in Alexandria where I'm partners with a law school classmate. We cover the county pretty well."

His eyes never stopped their mischievous dancing and he seemed to be thoroughly enjoying himself. Pirie found herself instantaneously attracted to his pleasant, non-malicious, teasing banter. He had none of Byron's dark, reckless good looks but he definitely had his own brand of quiet, warm appeal.

"You know that I'm one of your fans?" he asked, his eyes twinkling. "I've tried to follow your career as much as I could."

"Following my career must have taken a bit of doing," Pirie said a little ruefully. "One gets lost in the sea of show business very easily."

"I know what you mean," he laughed easily. "Lawyers have the same trouble. And they don't even have a guitar. Tell me, how's Philine?"

"Frankly, Adam, she's not well," Pirie answered. "That's why I came back." The girl noted that of all the people she had met this morning he had been one of the few to ask about Peely. Byron hadn't, and they had been much closer once. It said something about Adam Bailey, something she liked. She saw him glance at his watch and was sorry their meeting was about to end.

"I've an appointment," he said. "But maybe we can get together for a longer talk sometime."

"I'd like that," she said, surprising herself by the strength of her own feelings. He smiled—an assured, easy smile—and walked on as she clambered back into the battered little car. She hadn't accomplished what she'd come here to do, see Doc Gallagher, but the morning had been a pleasant, strengthening experience and she felt more confident as she headed back toward Moonwater. She could hope that perhaps Peely's condition would respond quickly to Doctor Gallagher's diagnosis. Perhaps she had let her imagination run away with her in general. She concentrated on hurrying back and she felt herself growing suddenly and terribly tired. The morning had relaxed her and now her physical exhaustion was making itself felt. When she reached the house she literally had to force herself to stay awake. She went to her room and showered and changed for dinner. The stinging needles of water, cold as she could stand it, helped to revive her, temporarily at least.

Dinner was served by Valonia in the main dining room and she sat opposite Peely, with Robert Barlow at the head of the big table. A tall candle in the centerpiece of the creamy-white Mandrake flowers moved fitfully in the hot air. Pirie saw that Peely seemed rested and brighter and they laughed and talked and took trips down memory lane to places and events of their childhood, not so far a trip for Peely. It was Peely who recalled how they used to each take one of the flat-bottomed wooden boats and play hide and seek amid the cypresses of the bayous, each rowing their own boat silently, stealthily, trying to catch the other by surprise. And it was Peely who suddenly exploded the happy normalcy of the conversation as she looked up at Pirie, accusingly.

"Last night you hid from me, again," she said. "I saw you disappear behind the big blackgum on the path to the bayou. I want you to promise me not to do that again."

Pirie held herself very still and her eyes flicked over to Robert Barlow's face and then to Valonia, who was clearing away the dishes. Both were impassive.

"When did you see me last night, Peely?" Pirie asked, quietly.

"When I woke up in the night," Peely replied. "You were heading down to the bayou and you disappeared in the trees. You were hiding from me, the way we used to do."

"Are you sure it was me you saw, hon?" Pirie asked. The girl nodded emphatically and looked up at Valonia, who was gazing at her with burning eyes. As the woman walked into the kitchen, Peely turned to her dessert, toyed with it a moment and Pirie saw that she was back in her own, curtained world. She made only desultory responses to Pirie's attempts at further conversation and then, suddenly, rose and went into the living room. Pirie could see the girl from the dining room and watched as she sat down at the old, grand piano. As Peely began to play, Valonia returned to stand at Robert Barlow's elbow. Peely's playing was a succession of dark chords, minor arpeggios and diminished fifths and sevenths, a mounting progression of dark, morbid music.

"Playing seems to relieve her," Valonia said. "Sometimes she'll play for an hour this way. Then I give her her medicine and she seems calmer, better again."

Pirie well knew the inner harmony, the personal comfort to be drawn from music, especially music made by oneself. To her, music had always been a reaching down inside oneself, cleansing, revealing, a highly personal interior communication, a kind of high Mass sung by the soul. Music could reveal the inner being, a reflection of the very essence of the soul, and this music of Peely's was tormented, anguished. It's rolling, dark, turgid sound told more of the girl's inner torture than any mere words could ever tell. And, while Peely continued to call forth the mournful sounds, Pirie turned to Barlow and Valonia.

"What is this business about her seeing me last night?" the girl asked, angrily, wondering if they had perhaps been telling Peely she had come and gone in a misguided effort to calm her nerves. "Have you been talking a lot about me or saying things which might make her dream she saw me?"

"No," Valonia answered at once. "She has been seeing your *ka*." Pirie met the piercing, burning gaze of the woman's eyes and felt the power that came from them.

"She saw my *ka*?" the girl repeated. "What are you talking about?"

"Your *ka* is your spiritual or astral double, provided for every mortal at birth," the woman answered. "We all have one, every one of us. It is the spiritual essence of your physical body. It is not visible to most of us, except at certain moments. But to those of us who tread upon the edge of another world, many things are visible. So it is with Peely."

Pirie felt her skin growing cold and damp. "You can't be serious," she said, swallowing hard. Valonia's stare never wavered and she held out a strong, thick finger, pointing it at the girl.

"You think your body is purely physical?" she asked. "When every minister and priest speaks of the spiritual side of the body? When even scientists admit that the body harbors chemical, electrical and magnetic impulses that vary with each person? Science itself uses electrical impulses to shock the mind, and the chemical make-up of the genes are still being studied by biochemists. Of course we each have a spiritual double, an electrochemical double of our physical self. The girl has seen your *ka*. It is as simple as that."

"You really believe this foolishness, don't you?" Pirie frowned, looking at Barlow and Valonia. "You both believe it."

"And you are a stupid little fool," Valonia said, savagely. "Tied down to your small, petty, restricted little mind."

Pirie saw the woman's huge hands tighten around the back of Robert Barlow's chair, the powerful fingers grow white as she pressed them hard against the wood. Pirie wanted to say more, to say that she'd never heard of anything so ridiculous, but the words stuck in her throat and she realized she was frightened. She wasn't sure of just what, though, the woman's obvious anger at being scoffed at or something less clearly defined. She breathed a sigh of relief when Valonia turned and abruptly went into the kitchen.

"Of course, you may believe what you wish to believe, Pierette," Robert Barlow spoke up, his smooth voice mellifluous and soothing. "Perhaps you can come up with another, more logical explanation for your sister's continuing reference to seeing you. Perhaps you would like to call them merely hallucinations."

His smile was coldly condescending. He was laughing at her, mocking her, and she felt her temper pushing through her fright.

"I'll find one," she said. "You can count on it." She saw his eyes narrow for an instant and thought it was hatred she saw in them but his smile was gracious and he dipped his handsome head in a curt nod.

"I hope you can, my dear," he said. "I look forward to your visit with Doc Asher. Perhaps he can talk to you on the practical level you can understand better."

The music stopped suddenly and Pirie got up and met her sister coming back into the room. The things she had heard were beyond her, but then so were Peely's haunted face and troubled, vacant eyes. Valonia appeared with a plain, unmarked bottle of medicine and a spoon and gave a portion to Peely with a quick, deft professionalism. The girl took it obediently.

"May I see the bottle?" Pirie asked, making her question more of a demand than a request. The woman handed her the bottle with an impassive face and Pirie unscrewed the cap. It had a bitter, acrid odor, unlike any medicine she had ever smelled. She handed Valonia the bottle and hurried after Peely who was already half-way up the stairs. As she put her arm around the younger girl's shoulder, Peely looked up and smiled and there was a sadness mingled with love in her eyes. Pirie felt her heart go out and as they entered the room she took her younger sister by the shoulders and looked deeply into her eyes.

"Now, you listen here, hon," she began. "If you want me, you just come to my room. If I'm not there, just wait there for me and I'll be back. There's not going to be anyone hiding."

"I'm so glad you're here, Pirie," the other girl said and Pirie hoped she had gotten through to her sister. It was hard to tell. Peely's wide, vacant eyes revealed little. She watched as Peely undressed and slipped on a nightgown. The girl's body was still smooth and sleek and maturing, she saw. Whatever terrible illness churned inside Peely, it had yet to extract a physical toll and for that she was happy. She left Peely stretched out on the bed in her nightgown, almost instantly falling into a deep sleep, and she was almost certain that the medicine Valonia had given her had contained some form of narcotic.

Pirie walked back to her own room and she felt completely exhausted. The temporary reprieve brought on by the shower had faded away and now the lack of sleep, the tension of the near-fatal accident, the shock at seeing Peely's condition all overwhelmed her with fatigue. She closed the door to her room and lay down on the bed in bra and panties and let the warm night breeze blow in through the window upon her. Lying there in the dark, she tried to sort out the events of the day but her mind refused to stay awake any longer. A jumble of dim words and images tumbled about in her mind... *Doctor Gallagher... Ka... Byron... Adam Bailey... Peely... Doc Asher.* The night air, heavy with mimosa, drifted into the room and hung over the sleeping figure atop the big bed. Pirie slept the sleep of the exhausted.

She hadn't any idea of how long she had been sleeping or what made her wake up when suddenly she found herself sitting bolt upright in bed, her skin bathed in cold perspiration.

Gripped in a sudden, nameless fright, only one thing leaped into her mind. Throwing on slacks and an overblouse, she ran barefoot from the room, down the carpeted corridor and into Peely's room. It was empty, staring back at her accusingly. Gasping, Pirie ran from the room and down the stairs and into the night. The moon, a day past three-quarters, lighted the lawn with its cold blue spell but just past the open area, the dense trees shut out its rays. The full moon and only the full moon could pierce their curtain. Moonwater had been well named. She raced across the grass, unmindful of the cold, wet dew that wrapped itself around her feet. All she could think of was Peely; Peely searching for her where she had "seen" her the night before, where they once played down by the bayou. She ran, brushed by low-hanging leaves and trailing streamers of moss, stumbling, falling and getting up again until she neared the edge of the dark, silent water that licked the mossy bank.

"Peely!" she called, fear in her voice. "Peely, I'm here. Are you looking for me? Over here, Peely."

Only the croak of a bullfrog answered and she ran the short distance to the very edge of the bayou and peered into the black water. It was at night that the 'gators came out and, worse than them, the water moccasins and copperheads. She knelt down and listened for sounds, noises she hadn't listened for in years, the soft slap of a swimmer in the water, the rustle of the ferns as legs brushed past it. Her eyes picked out the cypresses rising out of the water, ageless columns holding up a ceiling of hanging tentacles, twisted, tortured shapes. She called out again and once more listened for some answering sound but there was nothing. She rose to her feet, wet and cold in the damp moss at the edge of the bank, and suddenly she knew she was not alone. She whirled and saw the heavy pole, really a small log, hurtling at her, about to smash into her face. She threw herself backwards into the bayou, feeling the log graze her forehead as it hurtled by. It had been thrown at close range, from just behind the trunk of the blackgum, but there had been no chance to see who threw it. When she hit the water on her back she took a deep breath, went under and came up on the bank some ten feet below the spot where she'd gone in. She pulled herself out quickly, and anger mixed with fear as she crouched, waiting, listening. But there was no sound other than that of her own, hard breathing. Whoever had thrown the log at her had plenty of time to run while she was in the water. But, seizing her courage, she moved forward to the blackgum tree, to make certain. She picked up a small, flat rock on the way, holding it in her hand, now a tightly clenched fist. But, as she had thought, no one was there. Then and only then did her legs begin to tremble and she leaned against the trunk of the tree, letting the rock slip from her hand.

The terrible enormity of what had happened swept over her, wrapping itself around her wet body like an evil cape. Someone had tried to kill her. She repeated it to herself, unable to believe what she knew was true. If she hadn't sensed danger and turned, the log would have struck her in the back of the head and knocked her into the water unconscious. If she hadn't fallen prey to a hungry 'gator or a cottonmouth, she would surely have drowned and it would have been dismissed as a tragic accident. Just back after being away for three years, she had wandered out into the night, stumbled over a log perhaps, struck her head and fallen into the water. It had happened that way to others before. The bayous had more than their share of hapless victims over the years. It would have been neat, a perfect murder. She felt her wet body shiver in the night. Ordinarily, the cool of the water would have been welcome in the sultry heat of the heavy night air but she felt cold and clammy. Once again the wings of death had brushed past her. And Peely was still missing. She pushed herself from the tree and started back toward the house, knowing not what she would do but knowing only that she needed help. She tried to apply the force of calm reason as she hurried back through the dark, moving quickly through clutching trailers of moss and low-hanging vines. Who would want to kill her? It didn't make sense. And why? Of course, she thought instantly of Robert Barlow and Valonia. She was sure they disliked her as much as she disliked them. But dislike and murder are two different things. It could even have been a stranger, she reasoned. A poacher perhaps, afraid of being seen and recognized. Or an escaped convict afraid of apprehension. The bayous were known as a place for prisoners escaping from the prison farms to flee and to hide.

As she neared the house her fears for Peely pushed aside all thoughts of what had almost happened to her. She was surprised to see lights on in the living room and main foyer windows as she ran across the lawn to fling open the door, a wet, fearful figure in slacks and blouse. Peely was there, in her nightgown, along with Valonia, Barlow and old Thomas, the stableman.

"Pierette," Barlow exclaimed. "We were just about to go looking for you, too. What happened to you?"

"I fell into the bayou," Pirie answered, grimly. "I was running along the bank looking for Peely and slipped on a piece of wet moss."

Peely's eyes, round and confused, stared at Pirie and Valonia held the girl by the arm.

"We were afraid that's where you might have gone," the woman said. "When we checked Peely's room, as we have been doing, and found her gone, we immediately set out looking for her. Mr. Barlow went to your room to wake you so you could help but we found you had gone, too."

"Of course, we searched for Peely, first," Barlow added. "We found her behind the stables. Thomas, here, saw the lights on in the house and just came in to see if there was any trouble."

All perfectly reasonable explanations, Pirie heard herself thinking as her feet, cold and wet, dug into the carpet. She moved over and took Peely's arm.

"I'll put her to bed," she said and Valonia stepped back, forcing a smile. Pirie led her sister up the stairs and into her room. Once in the upstairs corridor, out of earshot, she spoke to the girl.

"Where did they find you, Peely?" she asked. "And why did you go out, again?"

"I don't know," Peely said, her voice catching. "I don't know anything about anything. I only know that when I woke up, Valonia was with me downstairs in the hall. I guess I wandered off, as they said. Maybe I sleepwalk or something."

"Poor Peely," the girl said, kissing her sister on the cheek. "We'll get you straightened out."

Peely sank down on the edge of the bed and Pirie pulled back the sheet and swung the girl's legs up onto the bed. As she did so, her hand brushed across the younger girl's feet and she almost gasped aloud. Peely's feet were warm and dry! Pirie repeated it again to herself. Not cold and wet from the night dew, as hers were, because the girl hadn't been outside at all. Like the slow tearing of a dark curtain, the truth of what had happened revealed itself to her. Peely had been taken from her room in the almost certain assumption that she, Pirie, would check on her during the night, find her gone and do just what she had done—rush out down to the bayou to search for her in the night. And there, someone had waited to kill her. Peely's absence from her room had been a lure. And it had almost worked. Moreover, had she not brushed the younger girl's warm, dry feet, she would never have known.

Peely was sleeping again and Pirie, closing the door softly and slowly, walked back to her room. Questions burned inside her, questions without answers. Questions that begged more questions and those had no answers, either. She had been a target for murder, cleverly contrived murder and she could no longer look away from Robert Barlow and the housekeeper, Valonia. They had obviously lied when they said they had found Peely out behind the stables. Was it they who had set up the lure and tried to murder her? All things pointed to them, except that she could supply no reason, no motivation. Inside her room she put on the heavy door latch and lay down on the bed after hanging up her wet clothes and drying her body. Of course there would be no going to Sheriff Whittaker with her story. It would be denied, scoffed at by both Barlow and Valonia, and it was no real evidence of anything, she knew. No doubt they'd even have a reasonable, logical explanation for Peely's feet being dry. And the attack upon her at the edge of the bayou could easily be dismissed as the overactive imagination of an overwrought girl. Or explained away as an attack by some fleeing convict. She herself had thought of that possibility. Barlow and Valonia would, too. No, Pirie told herself as she lay on the bed, she must have more than suspicions, more than personal bias to go on, and she recalled something her father had told her one time. Three rare *anhingas* or water turkeys had been slain on DuChamps land and her father had had trouble with a neighboring landowner at the time. He was trying to find out whether the rare birds had been slain by the spiteful neighbor, natural predators, poachers or thoughtless youngsters. It turned out to be poachers. "Never mistake facts for truth, Pirie," he had told her. "They're not necessarily the same thing. A lot of facts can point the wrong way. When you have only a few facts it's even more dangerous. Facts are only the building blocks that make up the structure called truth. They must be put together in the right way to build the structure."

Pirie stared at the dark and sought to sort out the facts so they could be put together. Twice now in twenty-four hours, death had reached out for her. Of course, the first time had been an accident, a freak occurrence, while the second one had been a clever attempt at murder. There could be no connection between the two. It was a ridiculous thought. But then why had she made the connection? She pressed her hands to her temples. Now she was being as far out as Valonia and her spiritual doubles. She had to put aside strange wonderings and concentrate on the facts. Someone had tried to kill her tonight. It could have been an escaped convict hiding in the bayou, afraid she might see him. But it had been Barlow and the woman, Valonia, who had told her the fake story about Peely having been found outside. And she would keep that fact secret, let them think their cleverness had been successful. She'd call Doc Gallagher in the early morning and get Peely to him. That had to come first, before anything else. Before, and she shuddered at the thought, there was another attempt at murder.

CHAPTER FOUR

In the morning the sun flooded into the room like a bright handclap to wake the sleeping girl. Pirie stretched, swung her long, slender legs out of bed and clad them in deep-blue slacks. She put on a blouse of soft pink and then went into Peely's room. The younger girl was almost dressed and seemed fairly bright. But the lost emptiness lurked just behind her eyes, waiting to take command at moment's opportunity. Pirie went down to breakfast with her sister, determined to be as falsely affable as she knew Robert Barlow would be. And she succeeded quite well, she thought, despite Valonia's grim, unsmiling face. At least the woman was more direct in her feelings, or perhaps merely less of an actor. Pirie hurried through breakfast and went out into the garden with Peely. In the warm sun of the morning the events of the night seemed like a bad dream, hardly to be believed. She watched Thomas walking from the stables with currycomb in hand, slowly ambling along. The grass was soft and the sun warm and it was a quiet, serene morning. But, Pirie knew, the serenity was a facade. Last night had happened. Someone had tried to kill her down at the bayou. And Valonia and Barlow had lied about Peely being out in the night. She gazed up and saw it was a cloudless sky, except that there were clouds, even if only she could see them. There were clouds and there was evil and something terrible lurking here at Moonwater. She turned abruptly and went into the hall to call Dr. Gallagher's office. The crisply professional voice of his nurse-receptionist answered.

"The Doctor has been detained in Cotile, an emergency at the hospital," the voice said. "He won't be back until Wednesday."

"Wednesday!" Pirie heard herself exclaim. "That's the day after tomorrow."

"Doctor Evans from Annaville will see all Dr. Gallagher's emergency cases till then," the nurse said. "Shall I schedule an appointment for you?"

"No, forget it," Pirie snapped. "I'll wait for Doctor Gallagher to get back." She slammed down the phone, furious, knowing her conversation had easily been heard in the dining room. Defiantly, she went in and faced Robert Barlow's undisguised disdain. Valonia, clearing away the dishes, was merely sternfaced.

"I take it you now understand why we preferred Doc Asher," Barlow intoned. Peely appeared at the doorway just then and Pirie, not trusting herself to answer even civilly, ignored Barlow and turned to her sister.

"We're going into town, you and I, hon," she said. "I think a little shopping spree would be good for us both."

"Oh, I'd like that." Peely brightened at once but it was a brightness which made Pirie's heart turn over. There was something childlike and detached in even this. She went upstairs with Peely while the girl changed into a pair of brown and blue plaid slacks, and took her purse. When the two girls went downstairs again Valonia was at the door, a little corsage in her hand.

"My, don't you look nice," she said to Peely, pinning the small red flowers onto the girl's blouse. "I just made this up quickly to help you look even nicer."

Peely's smile was open, grateful and Pirie felt almost ashamed of the mechanical grimace she managed. When they got into the car and drove off, she glanced at the corsage again. There were nine of the little red flowers and nine green little leaves. Unable to stop herself, she reached over, unpinned the corsage from Peely's blouse and threw it out the window, wincing at the outraged expression on the younger girl's face.

"Why'd you do that?" Peely asked, protest in her voice.

"I'm sorry," Pirie said grimly, wishing she really had a good explanation. "I was almost killed on the way here, a freak accident beside a big route sign marked nine. Those nine flowers made me think of it and they bothered me."

She was angry at herself for the attempt at logic to explain something entirely illogical and unexplainable and she was grateful, for a fleeting moment, that Peely wasn't her normal self. She would have hooted in derision if she were. As it was she only shrugged and gazed out the window.

They reached Grandview, parked and leisurely went from store to store. Pirie was happy to see Peely acting more and more like her old self. Of course, the wan, pallidness of her still remained but she wasn't so vacant, so empty-eyed. They stopped for lunch at the town's best, and only, tea room, and were just finishing when Pirie saw Adam Bailey come in. His smile was instant and warm as he came over to the table.

"Please sit down," Pirie said. "I'm sorry we're just about finished."

"I just popped in for a quick sandwich," he said. "It's good to see you both in town again together. Makes the old town look more like it should."

She was grateful for the moment as Peely, seeing an old schoolmate, excused herself to go across the restaurant. Adam Bailey's eyes followed the girl for a moment and then swung back to Pirie.

"Is Peely feeling better?" he asked and the abruptness of the question startled her.

"How did you know she was ill?" Pirie asked quickly, defensively.

"I didn't," Adam answered. "But looking at her makes it pretty obvious, doesn't it?" Pirie felt her lips purse. She shouldn't have been so suspicious so quickly. But then she was seeing shadows everywhere these days.

"I guess so," she said. "In fact, Peely is why I came back. I received a very disturbing letter from her."

"Has she been seeing a doctor?" Adam asked and she saw his eyes flick across the room, narrowing slightly, as he studied Peely as the girl talked with her friend.

"Mr. Barlow has had Doc Asher treating her," Pirie said, her eyes riveted on Adam Bailey's face, trying to catch some hint of a reaction. But his face remained a steady, unrevealing mask as he returned his gaze to her. And it was a mask, she sensed, and without knowing why she had the terrible urge to take him aside and tell him everything that had happened. But she didn't, of course. She hardly knew him, certainly not well enough to impose her problems on him. Yet there was a strength to the man, a comforting, reassuring quality to him that practically invited such imposition.

"I imagine you're a good counselor," she said, growing instantly embarrassed at having uttered such a complete *non sequitur.*

He smiled, that slow, warm smile that could embrace like a hug. "Thank you," he said. "But I'd like to know what prompted that remark."

"Nothing," she said, feeling her cream-white cheeks redden like a schoolgirl's. "I ... I don't know what made me say it."

"I think you do," he laughed, a deep, rich laugh. "But I'm glad you're not telling me."

"Why?"

"Because now I've an excuse to see you again and ask you about it," he grinned.

"Yes, I'd like that," she said, standing up, seeing that Peely was alone now and waiting forlornly in the doorway. "I'm afraid I've got to go now."

"Let's have that meeting soon," Adam Bailey said, his eyes suddenly serious, almost stern. "You're troubled about something. Maybe you'd like to talk about it."

"Does it show that much?" she asked. "I thought I was doing a good job of hiding it."

"You were," he said. "I'm just harder to hide things from than most people. A good lawyer gets a kind of feel for that sort of thing."

She left then, but took a moment to glance back through the window from outside to see Adam Bailey seated at one of the small tables, making it look even smaller. He was bigger than he seemed, one of those men who are so well put together their size comes only as an afterthought. She was happy at having met Adam Bailey just now. Unwarrantably, without justification, she felt as though she'd met a friend.

She and Peely shopped some more, refreshed by lunch, but by mid-afternoon Peely began to wilt rapidly. Peely, the practically inexhaustible bundle of energy. Her heart wrenched but the situation had its good side for the moment. Peely would be too exhausted to go wandering about tonight while she was out on her date with Byron Lee Hodges. She was still bothered about going off with Byron and leaving Peely alone with Valonia and Barlow. She'd see to it that they returned early, she promised herself. They got the car and turned toward home. The shadows were already dark as she drove the narrow road through the bayou land, and the slow-moving water and the dipping, hanging vines were beginning to assume their shapes of the night. But she could remember when it was fun to be frightened by them, when she and Peely would go out into the night and enjoy the thrills of terror. But of course the terror then had been a game inside themselves and they'd always been careful to stay away from the bayou proper at night where the real dangers waited. And now, there were no games and the terror waited all around. It wrapped itself around the girl like a cloak as she drew up before the ugly old house. To the right, past the house, the road opened further, deep into the back country where Doc Asher lived. Pirie shuddered. She'd traveled the old road countless times but now the mere thought of it was chilling. Damn, she said under her breath, angrily. She'd have to stop letting her imagination run off with her so.

Valonia opened the door and greeted them. "My, Miss Peely looks terribly tired," she said, disapproval in her tone. "I'll take up her upstairs and see that she gets her medicine right away. She's skipped the noonday dose today."

Pirie wanted to say no medicine but she held back. She had no reason to say so yet and it would only cause another scene. But she went to Peely's room a few minutes later and sat down on the edge of the bed where Peely lay stretched out, already changed into pajamas. Peely was very tired, it was plain, and her eyes had that vacant stare in them again.

"I'm going out for a while tonight, Peely," Pirie said. "With Byron Lee. But I'll be back early. No more walking around outside looking for me, promise?"

Peely nodded.

"You know I'm here now," Pirie continued. "I'll look in on you when I get back. If you want to see me you wait right here till then, understand?"

Peely attempted a small smile and nodded again.

"You know, you never did really see me wandering around outside," Pirie said gently. "That was all just your imagination."

"Oh, no," Peely said, sitting up, a small frown clouding her face. "I saw you, Pirie. I saw you. That's why I wrote you."

Pirie bit her lower lip. She wanted to shatter Peely's imaginings with the cold water of doubt at least.

"What was I wearing, hon?" she asked quietly. Peely thought for a long moment, so long that Pirie was about to say something else, when the girl answered suddenly. "The last time, it was a blue dress with a white and green stripe down the side," she said. Pirie felt her throat tighten and go dry. Peely had never seen that dress. No one here had. She'd bought it in New York and it was still at the bottom of her suitcase, unpacked. She had seen it there only this morning when she was searching for the pink blouse, and she'd made a mental note to finish unpacking her things. Peely had lain back down and was already asleep, eyes closed, her breathing slow, steady, deep. Pirie got up and walked slowly from the room, feeling almost dizzy, her fists clenched in tight, round little balls. It was impossible. Ridiculous. Black magic hocus-pocus. There had to be an explanation, a perfectly clear, reasoned explanation. Perhaps she had written Peely a letter describing the dress when she'd bought it. She'd written so many letters. It was certainly possible. She searched her memory, rummaging frantically through her mind, knowing all the while that she had never written such a letter.

In her room, Pirie eased herself down on the bed and sat silently for a long time, hearing Valonia's words echoing mockingly in her mind. Finally she got up and undressed to shower and change. It still was beyond understanding, making no sense. But then nothing seemed to make much sense now. Under the shower, letting the warmth of the water relax her tensed emotions, she tried to put aside the frightening, dark thoughts which defied sane understanding. She let the pure, physical pleasure of the shower help and vowed to enjoy the evening with Byron. But deep inside her, look away as hard as she might, she knew that the unanswered would one day have to be answered. Even if it were only with another question.

When Byron Lee arrived she was downstairs and waiting, wearing a gown of turquoise with thin, spaghetti straps that revealed the smooth, lovely roundness of her shoulders. Byron's look of appreciation was gratifying and his grin—that charming, tilted grin of his—had an extra measure of something in it. She took a moment to seek out Valonia in the kitchen.

"I've put a chair against the door of Peely's room," Pirie said, forcing herself to meet the woman's burning eyes. "You'll hear it if she tries to leave her room. That should eliminate any repetition of last night."

Valonia said nothing, nodding with her eyes only and Pirie left to join Byron outside.

"The Old Manse is still the best spot in the county," he said, spinning the convertible around to take the road back through Grandview. Even with Byron's smooth, bright chatter of things and places, the tangled bayous on each side of the road seemed to reach out to her ominously, a tangled echo of the twisted thoughts inside her. But she relaxed more as they reached the town, passed through it and finally drew up to the old mansion that had been converted to a stately restaurant. It was just as she had last seen it over two years ago, except that they'd added a small trio for dancing. With Byron holding her close, as he always did when they danced, the clock took giant leaps backwards. And not for her alone. "It felt good, Pirie," he said as they sat down. "It felt right."

She had to admit to herself that he was right, that she had enjoyed his touch, his arms around her. His grin, with that rakish tilt to it, was too infectious not to draw a reply from the heart. But in her two years away she had learned to separate real desire from sentimentality and nostalgia and so they talked about many things and danced some more and laughed a lot. Byron Lee was too handsome, too charming, too completely male to resist and it was only natural that old feelings should stir again in her, she told herself. It was also natural that when they went out into the gardens behind the restaurant that his lips should find hers. He was a unique combination of southern Louisianan courtliness and modern urban sophistication and she felt her lips responding to his, responding too eagerly. She pulled away, with more effort than she should have needed, she realized in annoyance at herself. Mockingly, that little question popped up in her mind again. Why had she walked away from Byron two years before? Oh, she had wanted a career, but that really wasn't reason enough. Byron's hand holding hers, leading her back to their table, made her kick aside the question as an unwarranted intrusion.

As they finished dinner, it was she who brought up Peely, seeking some outside viewpoints that might help her see things better.

"Glad you mentioned Peely," Byron said quickly. "That's something I was going to get around to talking to you about tonight."

Pirie's gratification at his instant interest vanished with something of a sour taste as he went on.

"I've been dabbling in real estate," Byron Lee said. "And I've a buyer for Moonwater, a client who'll pay a good price. But he wants a quick sale. I was going to get your address to write you when there you were in town suddenly."

"I can't sell Moonwater," Pirie said, feeling very letdown and annoyed with herself for feeling that way. But it was very plain that Byron's interest in Peely had been commercial and nothing more. "You know it's Peely's, Byron Lee," she reminded him. "You know my father left it to her. I remember talking to you about that when he died."

"Yes, but you're trustee for her," Byron Lee said, his tilted little smile ingratiating. "You could get her to sell. All you'd have to do is convince her she'd be getting a good price for it and I know that wouldn't be hard, not for you."

"I can't," Pirie said. "I promised Daddy I'd see to it that Moonwater stayed hers until she was eighteen, when she'd be old enough to make a decision on her own. That's what he wanted. It wouldn't seem right to talk her into selling, especially now."

"Why especially now?" Byron Lee asked.

"Because Peely hasn't been well," Pirie said, more sharply than she intended to. "Don't tell me you haven't noticed. She's in no state to think clearly about anything."

"That's all the more reason you should do her thinking for her," Byron said and Pirie saw he was having some difficulty maintaining his air of urbane charm. Suddenly she wondered, was that why she'd been able to walk away two years ago? Was it because Byron Lee's very real charm nonetheless masked a person more self-involved than anything else?

He ordered another round of drinks, "after-dinner pick-me-ups" he called them, but they didn't do much because he grew moodily silent. He kept returning to his offer and urging Pirie to consider it and it wasn't till they were driving back to Moonwater that his usual ebullience returned. Unexpectedly, as they stopped outside the house in the dark shadows of a big acacia, his lips were on hers, demanding, almost rough. She felt herself responding again to his animal sensuousness. Byron had always been like that, able to reach anyone with that part of himself if in no other way. Finally she managed to pull away and knew it was not Byron but herself she'd had to fight to do so. This was no time for an affair with Byron Lee, not yet, anyway. Things were disturbed and unsettling enough without adding more to her already strained emotions. Besides, something told her that her response to Byron had been more that of a need to find some refuge. That and a physical response and she'd long ago learned the unsatisfying hollowness of that hiding place. As he stood by the car he smiled at her again.

"Think about what I said," he commented. "Forget that Peely exists."

"But she does exist!" Pirie shot back, shocked by his remark.

"Not really," he said. "If she's mentally ill she doesn't exist in a rational way. You have to exist for her. Think about it."

Pirie turned and went into the house, into the dark wood of the foyer and immediately felt it close around her, not protectively as a house should, but suffocatingly. Light broke into the darkness of the foyer, harshly, shattering the dark, as the kitchen door opened and Valonia stood there. Almost silhouetted, with the light behind her, she looked like a figure from some other world, towering, gaunt, forbidding.

"Peely's been asleep all evening," the woman said. "She's all right. I've looked in on her."

It was a subtle order for Pirie not to bother but the girl defied it angrily. "I'll look for myself," she snapped and felt the woman's hatred as she brushed past her. Her temper was something for which Pirie was grateful. It helped get her over the fears that ordinarily might have frozen her into abject inaction. As she went upstairs, she wished that it were only anger and hate and fear she had to deal with in this old house for those were at least tangible things. But this house held intimations of things unknown, of powers and forces beyond her comprehensions, at least. Looking in on Peely, seeing the girl asleep, brought back the words of their last talk with renewed clarity. Pirie put the chair back against the door and went to her room, undressing quickly and slipping into bed. But sleep stayed out of her reach as she thought of the day's events, Peely's insistence about seeing her in the night, her perfect description of the dress, Byron Lee's talk of her selling Moonwater. Nothing had happened as it should have, except that brief visit with Adam Bailey. Everything else turned out to be an exercise in the unexpected. Maybe Byron Lee was right, she thought to herself. Maybe she should sell Moonwater to his client. She thought about his last words to her. Maybe they made more sense than she wanted to admit. Peely certainly wasn't existing in a rational way and if she didn't improve, the decisions would fall upon her own shoulders sooner or later. But if Peely wasn't rational, if she were deeply disturbed, how was she able to see that dress so clearly? "She saw your Ka." The voice floated into her mind, Valonia's voice, and Pirie angrily rejected it again. She would do nothing, take no action on anything, until she saw Doctor Gallagher. She would close no doors, nor open any, till then. Turning on her side, she forced herself to think of the nice part of the evening, of the fun she had had with Byron Lee, of the touch of his lips on hers, and finally she fell asleep, a fitful, tossing-turning sleep, but sleep. She was young, and as her body fought its own fight to recharge itself, the night finally passed into day with nothing more to disturb the girl. But when morning came, she knew that only night had passed and nothing else.

CHAPTER FIVE

Peely seemed refreshed in the morning, too, and the girls delayed their own breakfast and ate together later, after Robert Barlow had finished. It was mid-morning and they were walking toward the stables when Byron Lee's convertible swung into the front drive. An arm reached up swinging a picnic basket, followed by Byron Lee brandishing a long loaf of French bread in the air like a sword. Wearing a double-breasted blue blazer with brass buttons and an open-necked shirt, his tilted, boyish smile was never more appealing, his reckless, dark good looks never more exciting.

"I decided you both needed a picnic," he called out. Pirie glanced at Peely and saw the girl's eyes shine. The idea was more than a little appealing to her, too. Anything that would keep Peely from Moonwater and the influence of Valonia and Barlow appealed to Pirie. They quickly clambered into the car and in minutes they were speeding back through town and out beyond, almost to the very edge of bayou country where a hillside sloped steeply and a small stream glistened in the sun. Peely had a fine time in the brightness of the day, though she rested often, her energy still a thing of short spurts, and Byron Lee found time to kiss Pirie more often than she really wanted. But once again she felt the compelling sexuality of Byron Lee as he pressed down upon her in the grass and that, too, brought back memories.

"About what I said last night, Pirie," he said to her. "Maybe I was kind of rough on you. I still want you to sell Moonwater to me for my client but I've been thinking about Peely. You ought to check into her condition more before you sell, I guess. You ought to go visit Doc Asher."

"You, too?" Pirie frowned.

"Well, you said he's the one they've had treating her," Byron Lee protested. "You ought to talk to the man, especially if you're going to see Doctor Gallagher tomorrow."

Seeing Pirie's little frown, he went on quickly. "For your own good, I mean. You want to be able to tell Doctor Gallagher as much as you can, don't you? Maybe you can find out what Doc Asher's been giving Peely as medicine. Find out for yourself what his diagnosis is. Even if he really hasn't got one you can tell that to Doctor Gallagher. Go out there, let Doc Asher tell you whatever he can. Then you'll be more prepared when you see Gallagher tomorrow."

He was making sense, Pirie saw, good sense. The more she knew, the more she could tell Doctor Gallagher, the more it might help him in his own examination of Peely. And, it seemed, Byron Lee Hodges was trying to make up for his insensitivity of the previous night; she felt warm and grateful for that.

"I've got a four o'clock meeting," he said," and I've got to get you all back to Moonwater first. You'll have a few hours left in the afternoon. Go see Doc Asher. Find out what you can from him."

Pirie nodded, deciding to do it. There'd be time and it made sense the way Byron had presented it to her. Besides, she knew she'd been letting her dislike of Valonia and Robert Barlow get in the way of her own logic. They gathered up picnic papers and remains and climbed back into the car. She felt better than she had at any time since getting Peely's letter in New York. Tomorrow she'd be seeing Doctor Gallagher and the world would be a better place. Somehow, all the unexplainable, unaccountable things would fall into place in a sane, reasonable way. She refused to let herself think otherwise, certainly not when now, for the first time, she was experiencing the reassuring glow of confidence. She'd take Barlow's smug arrogance when she announced she was going to visit Doc Asher. Let him think what ever he would.

It was only three o'clock when they returned to Moonwater and Peely went to her room, her energies thoroughly depleted by the morning's fun. Pirie phoned Doc Asher to tell him she was coming out to see him and Barlow's face was, as she had told herself it would be, superior and arrogant. It was Valonia's face that bothered the girl. The woman's piercing eyes held a strange, almost triumphant light and Pirie felt a tremor pass through her body. The woman's eyes seemed to be growing more and more demoniacal. Or was that just more of her active imagination, Pirie asked herself. She didn't stop to change but went directly to the stables where Thomas was grooming the horses. To reach Doc Asher's meant taking the narrow back roads of the bayous where only horse and rig could go. Thomas hitched up the buckboard and she flicked the reins over the horse's rump. She ducked her head as the wagon went through the small passage at the right of the house, a mere hole in the wall of greenery and vines and in moments she was riding through the dank, damp world of the back country. This was primitive land, not harsh like some primitive lands, but softly menacing, replete with unexpected turns and bayous, deadly, grasping marshes and mud flats masked by the sawgrass. Black Mangroves towered over dense tangles of aerial roots, and the day only filtered down to the land. The bullfrogs were a constant chorus in the silence of this world within a world, this primeval place where time had stood still. She slowed her horse as memory held the reins and they approached the narrow bridge of wide wood planks that crossed the place called Thompson's marsh, a deadly mire of quicksand and sucking mud. She had passed over it often enough with her father when he investigated the land parcels beyond the back country. The road narrowed further and the bridge came into view. Pirie was beginning to wish she hadn't decided to come after all. But the buckboard crossed the small bridge of planks and she continued on.

It was a measure of the man that he chose to live out here in the backwater country. Of course, he claimed it was to make himself available to the trappers, Indians and primitive families of the area who grubbed a meager life from the bayous. They were scattered throughout the deep, dense back country. But Doc Asher had his patients in Grandview, too, mostly old women and people from the back lands. The road curved and suddenly opened to reveal a low, flat house, log and planking, Doc Asher's combined home and office. Doc Asher came to the door as the girl climbed from the buckboard. Of course, she'd only seen the man passing in town but he was as she remembered—lean, spare, with quick, ferret-like movements. He wore steel-rimmed glasses and his hair was quite black for a man his age, she noted. She'd never noticed how bright blue his eyes were, though.

"I expected you would be visiting me before this, my dear," Doctor Asher said, leading the girl into a cluttered, unkempt living room. She saw another room beyond, with an examination table and rows of dusty bottles and gallon jugs lining the walls.

"Perhaps I should have," Pirie remarked. "I certainly want to know what Peely's illness is, or at least your diagnosis of it." She hadn't meant to sound so skeptical but she saw the man had caught the import of her tone at once. His eyes, darting, held still for a moment and seemed to grow smaller.

"Your sister's illness is not easy to diagnose," he said. "I would say it has mental and metaphysical roots."

"Is Peely subject to hallucinations?" Pirie asked.

"The term hallucinations is itself much misused," Doc Asher answered, pressing the tips of his fingers against one another.

"Does she see things that aren't there?" Pirie asked, feeling her own impatience gathering. The man smiled, a short, fleeting smile that went with his darting eyes.

"To answer that we must first know whether a thing really is or isn't there," he said. "We might even have to first define the meaning of existence."

Pirie's lips tightened and she snapped out what Valonia had said about Peely seeing her "ka."

"I'd say that was seeing things," Pirie snapped.

"Once again, my dear, you mean seeing something that wasn't there," Doc Asher said. "But each day we learn new things about the chemistry of our bodies. It is an established medical fact that the electrical impulses within our minds and our bodies emit waves of their own. I believe those waves are wholly and totally individual, attuned to our own, individual genetic linkage."

"Are you saying you believe this rot about having an astral double?" Pirie exclaimed. "Are you saying we each emit special waves of our physical self that can be seen?"

Doc Asher's smile was deprecating. "I did not say that exactly," he answered. "I merely said that I do not believe this would be impossible. Of course, your astral double could only be seen by someone capable of extreme metaphysical concentration and perhaps uniquely attuned to you."

Pirie didn't bother to disguise the look of shock and disbelief she knew flooded over her face. The man was in effect saying he believed in Valonia's wild talk about her "ka." He was being more clever, hedging more, but that's what it amounted to in essence. Of course such things were pure rubbish, utter rot. Even if Peely did somehow, someway, describe that dress perfectly. She looked up, lost in her own angry thoughts for a moment, to see Doc Asher studying her intently.

"You do not believe in paranormal experiences, my dear?" he smiled. At the look of puzzlement in her eyes he went on to explain, "A paranormal experience is one that goes beyond our ordinary range of sensory experiences but that will, in time, have a perfectly reasonable or scientific definition as our knowledge increases. Extrasensory perception, clairvoyance, these are paranormal experiences."

"I believe in flashes of clairvoyance, in people having a sudden insight of extra-sensory perception," Pirie said. "But having astral doubles is going a long way beyond that. Having an image made up of reflected electrical waves or impulses is a bit much, I think."

Doc Asher shrugged. "Everything is a bit much when we do not understand it or it's possibilities frighten us." He smiled benignly and Pirie felt her temper soar.

"What kind of medicine have you been giving my sister?" she asked bluntly. A stubborn wariness crept into the little doctor's eyes.

"I'm afraid I cannot divulge that, except to tell you that it is medicine expressly made for your sister's problems," he said. "Your attitude tells me you would not be able to understand the elements basic to my approach in this matter."

"And your attitude tells me that I was right all along. You're nothing but an old fraud," Pirie shot back angrily. "A fraud and a fake, as big a believer in occult idiocy and black magic as Valonia and Barlow."

The girl got to her feet and stalked from the little house in fury. It was much safer to hold onto her fury than to contemplate the possibility that there could be any shred of truth to the little man's stand. Darkness was moving quickly to settle upon the bayous and she wanted to be back at Moonwater before that happened. All her suspicions about Doc Asher had been confirmed, she told herself smugly. He was not only a fraud but worse, a clever manipulator of old superstitions and ancient beliefs, practicing a twentieth-century brand of pseudoscientific witchcraft. Him and his paranormal experiences, she snorted, taking a curve too fast and feeling the rear wheels of the buckboard skitter wildly along the edge of the road. She slowed the horse a little but only a little. The road was narrowing again. The bridge over Thompson's marsh was coming up and she reined in. The horse followed the path as it narrowed to the wooden bridge and then, suddenly, pitching her forward and almost off the seat with its unexpectedness, the animal came to a stiff legged halt less than a foot from the bridge.

Pirie snapped the reins over the horse's back and the horse took a step backwards.

"No, not that way," Pirie exclaimed, impatiently angry. She brought the end of the reins down on the animal's rump and the horse snorted but refused to move forward.

"Come on, now," Pirie said through gritted teeth, yanking on the reins for emphasis. The horse shook itself and pawed the ground with its right hoof.

"Dammit," Pirie swore, jumping from the buckboard. She knew horses. The DuChamps had always had a stable and she'd learned about the stubbornness of a horse at an early age. She knew how some little thing could make them balk and shy away—a leaf, a shadow, a piece of paper sometimes. Whatever had done it now she knew she'd have to lead him past the spot. She seized the bridle and pulled. The horse threw his head up and she yanked down hard to keep her grip. She pulled again, getting a firmer grip on the noseband and again the horse resisted, pulling back. Angrily, Pirie yelled at the animal and stepped back to brace her left foot on the first plank of the little bridge. She half-screamed as the plank upended and she fell to one knee, clinging to the horse's bridle with one hand. She saw the plank teeter and then slide down to fall into the quicksand of the marsh below. Hearing the thump of her heart beating wildly, she pulled herself to her feet and reached out with one foot to touch the second wide plank. It moved easily, sliding to one side instantly as she pushed against it with her toe. She knelt down and then lay flat on the ground, peering under the little bridge. In the fast-fading light she saw that the wooden supports of the first four planks had been removed. There was nothing holding the planks in place. If she'd gone over the bridge either the horse or the buckboard would have dislodged them and she would have been pitched into the sucking marsh below.

Pirie got up and stood very still while she drew her breath in slowly and then let it out in a deep sigh. The cold perspiration soaking through her blouse wasn't what made her shiver. It was the cold wings of death that brushed past her in defeat. She put her hand up automatically and caressed the soft warmth of the horse's snout. Frightening, sickening realization swept over her and she felt weak, almost dizzy. The attempt to kill her had been clever, arranged so it would seem an accident, the buckboard running off the bridge, tearing up some of the planks in the process. Her body, in the depths of the quicksand and mud of the marsh, might never have been found. And, even more terrifying, it had to have been done while she was at Doc Asher's place. The bridge had been perfectly all right when she'd passed on her way to visit the doctor. And death would have had its victim, except for the horse's refusal to set foot on the bridge. Now, ironically, she had to recognize that her life had been saved by an act beyond ordinary explanation. Some would call it instinct, in this case the mysterious sensitivity of animal instinct, the sense of danger when there is no danger to be seen or heard or smelled. Some would call it that but she knew what Doc Asher would call it—a paranormal experience, an occurrence beyond our knowledge, not to be explained in any rational terms. And of course there was no denying what had happened, there was no doubting this paranormal experience. The animal, with an instinct beyond its normal sensory abilities, had experienced the inner warning of danger. Children had been known to experience the same irrational signals from deep in their inner psyche, she knew, and so had some adults at certain times. She had to admit the fact and now the frightening questioning immediately leaped out at her, refusing to be put aside any longer. If one paranormal experience can exist, why not two, or three, or more? Why not Valonia's astral double, the "ka?" But with almost reflex action, Pirie pulled the force of rational logic to her defense. The proven existence of one kind of paranormal activity didn't automatically prove the reality of every other kind. But her logic proved less than satisfying as she knew, deep inside herself, that she was only using it to avoid facing that which terrified her by its dark and unknown quantities. Angrily pushing all such thought aside, she turned to the very clear facts that were frightening enough. Someone had tried to kill her again and there was nothing extra-sensory about that. It had been the second attempt to kill her, the second time she had escaped death by inches. The log hurtling at her down by the bayous flashed in front of her eyes for a second.

She climbed back into the buckboard. She would have to search for the other tortuous, circuitous back roads that wound around the marsh. Night had closed on the bayous as the girl made her way slowly, fearfully, through dead-end passages and paths overgrown with vines and tendrils and all manner of clutching things.

Every hanging shape, every gnarled branch, every trailing tendril seemed to reach out for her and every sudden noise was a mocking, fearful laugh at this alien in the night. Unseen sounds were all around her—crackling sounds, scurrying and slithering sounds, crawling, bumping and snapping sounds and they stayed with the girl and the buckboard as she moved through the winding, seemingly aimless paths. She held herself stiff-backed in the seat, hands clenched tight around the reins, the horse finding its own way more often than not. She tried to ignore the sounds of the unseen creatures and the leaves that blew when there was no wind. But there was no ignoring the conspiracy of the night against her intrusion. It was as real and powerful a force as the others that had been loosed upon her. But she could refuse to give in and that's what she did, plodding onward, somehow finding the road on which she'd come and turning the buckboard toward Moonwater.

She had been gone hours and when she drew up before the house, Thomas ran from the stables, real concern on his face. "I was going to call Sheriff Whittaker soon," he said, helping Pirie to the ground. She clung to the man's arm for a moment, gathering the strength to walk into the house. She didn't have much more than that left, she knew, and her clothes were soaked from perspiration and the dank humid air of the bayous. Valonia opened the door of the house and came out with Robert Barlow close behind her. They, too, showed concern and anxiety at her late return and professed their intention of calling the Sheriff in "another ten minutes." Pirie said nothing. There was nothing she could or would say. She didn't even have the strength to study their faces. She went into the house and paused to ask about Peely.

"She's asleep," Valonia said, her face growing stern. "And she ought to be, considering what she did."

Pirie felt her pulse quicken even through the utter exhaustion of her body. "What do you mean?" she asked the woman.

"After you left, Peely went to the stables, took one of the horses and raced away on it," Valonia said.

"We all know Peely's an excellent rider," Barlow cut in, "but in her present condition there was no telling what she might do. She was gone for almost two hours. Thomas and I saddled up and tried to find her but he had no luck. She came back finally with the horse all lathered up from long, hard riding. She wouldn't tell us where she'd been. She claimed she didn't really know."

"I gave her some medicine and put her to bed," Valonia said. Pirie felt herself awaying and she closed her eyes for a moment, gathered herself and turned away, climbing upstairs slowly. Despite her fatigue, she looked in on Peely. The girl was in a deep sleep and Pirie stumbled into her room, locked the door and undressed while lying on the bed. She slipped under the sheets naked, feeling their smooth, comforting touch against her body. There was so much to unravel, so much to think about, to try to figure out. But not now, she murmured to herself. Peely had run away, her mind noted dazedly. Maybe they deliberately let her do so to have the time alone to follow the buckboard? But Peely had returned safely and that was good. There were more thoughts but she was too exhausted to think about them. Sleep came—wonderful, comforting sleep that shut out the world.

CHAPTER SIX

Pirie woke early, as the first, gray light of day pushed away the night. She lay in bed, her mind quickly alert, perhaps because it had never really slept. Before the others rose, before the day properly began, she would make her plans, for one thing was clear above all else: time was running out for her. Twice now, deliberate attempts on her life had been made. Twice now, she had cheated death. The freak accident on the highway couldn't be counted. Or could it? Why did it keep coming back to her so persistently? All this talk of occult phenomena, of paranormal experiences, was getting to her, she told herself impatiently. But it was crystal clear to the girl that the attempts on her life would be followed by another one. The failure of the first ones made that much a certainty.

She got up and showered, letting the warm needles of water stimulate her mind as well as her skin. The killer (or killers, she added grimly), had indeed been clever, but only a very few people knew she had gone to visit Doc Asher. The killer had to be one of them. Robert Barlow and Valonia knew that was where she had gone. And of course Byron Lee and Peely had known, but she dismissed those two at once. Robert Barlow or Valonia had followed after her, waited till she'd crossed the bridge and then prepared it for her fatal "accident" as she returned from her visit to Doc Asher. But why did they want to kill her? Was there some connection with Peely's condition? Or were she and Peely just in the way of something else? As the questions revolved in her mind, the girl realized that she had only strong suspicions, not facts, and she frowned to herself as she started to dress. She never knew facts were so elusive, so difficult to come by. She didn't have the faintest motivation that could support her suspicions about Barlow and Valonia, she realized with increasing bitterness. The more she examined what she knew, the more she realized that only two facts were firmly in her possession. One, that someone had tried to kill her and two, that only four people knew she'd gone to visit Doc Asher and that she'd be crossing the bridge over Thompson's marsh. A wave of dejection swept over her. She really hadn't anything solid that would convince anyone of anything. She'd intended calling Sheriff Whittaker to report the condition of the bridge, anyway, and now she had a second reason and she hurried down to the hall phone. It was still very early but Sheriff Whittaker was always in the office first thing in the morning and she heard his flat, unemotional voice. She told him, words rushing from her in a torrent, of how she'd found the bridge supports gone and had almost been killed.

"But the bridge had been all right when I passed over it an hour earlier," she added, waiting to her his reply. It was frustratingly expected when he answered in his slow, flat way of speaking.

"You were just plumb lucky then, Miss Pirie," the Sheriff said. "That bridge isn't hardly used much and those supports probably just wore away. But I'll get Sam Hodge out there to fix it right away. I appreciate your calling me on it."

Pirie put down the phone quietly. Under other circumstances she might even have smiled; it had so thoroughly turned out as she had guessed it would. Sheriff Whittaker wouldn't see it as anything but a perfectly ordinary set of circumstances. He wouldn't see it as a diabolically clever attempt at murder. He just wasn't geared to thinking that way. Things like that didn't happen in Grandview County. Oh, once in a while someone killed someone else but that was always over an argument or some woman. Killing in this land, to Sheriff Whittaker, at least, was a simple, uncomplicated thing. She could just see his skeptical, lean face with his eyebrows rising higher and higher as she tried to convince him differently. No, Sheriff Whittaker would need evidence before he'd act—hard, unvarnished, tangible evidence. But she had none of that, Piri knew, and she wondered how she could get it before her luck ran out. Those out to kill her were determined as well as clever.

As she stood by the phone, Valonia came down the stairs, her long, gray dress making small rustling sounds on the stairs as she walked down them.

"You're up early, Pirie," she grunted, fastening the girl with a hard stare. Pirie returned it defiantly.

"I've a lot to do today," she answered, brushing past the woman as she went up the steps to Peely's room. Peely was awake, sitting up in bed, as Pirie entered her room.

"I'm not coming down for breakfast," Peely announced immediately, a sullenness in her face.

"Why not?" Pirie asked, trying to sound bright and casual.

"I don't feel like it. I'm tired. I hurt," Peely said.

"Maybe too much hard riding yesterday," Pirie offered. "Where did you go, hon?"

"I don't know," Peely said crossly. Pirie watched as the girl laid her head back against the pillows propped up at the head of the bed. Her blue eyes were starting to stare vacantly again.

"Has Valonia been in to see you already this morning?" Pirie asked and her sister nodded.

"Did she give you more medicine?" Pirie pressed.

"Yes," Peely said and Pirie turned on her heel, grim anger coursing through her body. She was at the door when Peely called to her in a small, lost voice, all the cross sullenness gone from her.

"Don't be mad at me, Pirie," she said and the older girl gave her a warm, reassuring smile. Peely lay back and closed her eyes and Pirie shut the door behind her. She practically raced down to the phone, disregarding the fact that it was still early in the morning. Her hands shook with anger and inner hurt and she saw Peely's wan, staring, disturbed little face swimming before her as she dialed Doctor Gallagher's number. Robert Barlow paused at the entrance to the dining room and nodded pleasantly to her. The girl barely acknowledged the gesture. Deceit, hypocrisy, these things had never been part of her and and she couldn't make them so now, even though she had tried to mask her feelings. Her heart leaped as she heard Doctor Gallagher's deep, avuncular voice answer the phone.

"Oh, yes, Pierette, I saw the message that you'd been trying to get me," he said. "It's good to have you back with us again."

She cut short the polite talk and tried to hold her voice steady.

"I've come back because something terrible is wrong with Peely," she said. "Can you come out and look at her, Doctor Gallagher? I think it would be good if you could see her here and watch her for a while."

"Hmmmm," Doctor Gallagher murmured and Pirie could imagine him pouring over his calendar pad, his short, gray hair and his round, kind face clearly outlined in her mind. "I just got back today and things are crowded. What's more, my nurse has the afternoon off."

"Oh, my," Pirie murmured in sympathy. "Couldn't she take some other afternoon off?"

"She should have gone yesterday. Death in the family," Doctor Gallagher replied. "So now that I'm back she has to go. But you sound very troubled, young lady. I think I could get out to see you around five this afternoon."

"Five this afternoon?" Pirie exclaimed, almost shouting it out in relief. "Oh yes, wonderful."

"It's been a long time since I've been out there to your place," the Doctor said, thinking aloud. "I hope I can remember the way."

"Why don't I meet you at the main fork in the road just outside Grandview?" Pirie said quickly. "That way I can lead you back here and we won't have to worry about your getting lost."

The physician agreed quickly and so it was arranged; the girl put down the phone with a feeling of triumph. Peely's illness might be only one element in the dark web of evil that encircled Moonwater. The attempts on her life might be entirely unrelated but somehow she didn't think so. She couldn't tell herself why she didn't think so and she felt a wry smile cross her face. Was it a sixth sense? An extra-sensory knowledge? After Doctor Gallagher diagnosed Peely's trouble she'd find time to sit down and talk with him about paranormal experiences.

She passed Valonia and Barlow at breakfast and didn't pause. She wanted to talk to Thomas and went directly to the stables. Perhaps Peely had said something to him when she returned yesterday. Poor, confused, upset, ill Peely. Things would soon be better for her, Pirie told herself confidently. Thomas, sweeping out a stall, looked up as Pirie entered and tipped his battered old felt hat. But he had little to tell about Peely's ride except that she had come back "looking wild-eyed and mighty strange."

"You know, Miss Pirie, your sister has been awfully funny-acting lately," Thomas said, hesitant about speaking out on matters none of his concern. "In fact," he added, "I been noticing that for some while."

"I know, Thomas," she said. "And I'm going to do something about it."

"Mr. Barlow and Valonia were mighty concerned about her yesterday, too," Thomas said. "They didn't leave the place all afternoon. They just kept coming down here to see if she'd come back, first one, then the other."

Thomas's words came to her with a delayed impact and then, suddenly, she felt as though she'd been dropped into a vat of ice water. If Barlow and Valonia hadn't left the place all afternoon, who had fixed the bridge so she would be plunged into the marsh? Pirie turned and walked to the house, moving as though she were in a daze. Only two other people knew where she was going, Peely and Byron Lee. When she reached her room, Pirie felt sick, physically ill as she forced herself to face the shocking thoughts that filled her mind. Peely had been gone for some two hours, they had said, more than enough time to have followed her, fixed the bridge and returned. *No,* Pirie heard a voice cry out within her, *no,* and she stared dully into space, seeking some way in which to turn from the ugliness of her thoughts. But there was no way to turn from them, no way at all. Peely was unquestionably ill, and the illness had some form of emotional or mental base, perhaps both. Could she harbor an imagined hatred for her, spawned in some twisted, warped darkness of the mind? It was more than just possible, shattering as the thought might be. Such things had happened before, she knew, the mentally ill turning first on those they most cared about. Peely might have written the letter to lure her back. If she were going to explore this train of thought she had to explore every angle of it, she realized. And at the bayou, the log could have been flung by Peely. If she had worn shoes her feet would have stayed warm and dry. The mentally disturbed, she had often heard said, could be terribly, terribly clever.

Pirie shuddered, her heart being torn asunder by her own thoughts. Was there truth in those thoughts? Or was she doing a frightful disservice to Peely? Barlow and Valonia could have hired someone to follow her and fix the bridge. Now there was a thought she could warm to without inner repercussions and she enjoyed the glow of it for a few moments. And then there was Byron Lee Hodges. But of them all, Byron had no reason, no motive. Or did he? Was getting the house for his client that all-important? It seemed beyond belief, but then she was learning at every turn how little was really beyond belief. What if it were that vital to Byron to acquire the house, Pirie asked herself. If she were out of the picture and Peely adjudged mentally incompetent, Robert Barlow would be easy to deal with. So they all had reasons, reasons she could bring herself to outline but not to believe. Ironically, Robert Barlow and Valonia stood without any clear motives and yet to Pirie they were the prime suspects. They were, to the girl, possessed of an evil that far outdistanced reasoned areas such as motivation. But, despite her firm beliefs, she knew that reason and not emotion would have to be the final judge. As if from far away she heard her name being called and she shook herself loose of the jumbled world of fears and doubts and suspicions into which she had gone. It was Valonia, calling her from downstairs.

"Telephone for you, Pirie," the woman was calling and the girl hurried down to take the call.

"Hello," the voice on the other end said, warm and rich. "I wondered if you might be coming into town. I thought we might have that little talk we promised ourselves."

"Adam Bailey," Pirie cried in genuine pleasure. "It's good hearing from you. But I can't, not today. I'm staying around till later when I'm meeting Doctor Gallagher about Peely."

"Glad to hear that," Adam Bailey said. "We'll make it next time. I'll call you."

"Please do, Adam," Pirie said, once again surprising herself with the instant warmth the man aroused in her. When she put down the phone she turned to see Peely there, her eyes wide, questioning.

"I'm going to see Doctor Gallagher?" the girl asked and Peely took her sister's arm.

"He's coming here to see you late today," Pirie explained. "I'm going to meet him and bring him back. I'd like him to have a look at you." Pirie watched the younger girl intently, searching her face for any sign of the resentment of sullen crossness she had shown that morning. But Peely merely shrugged and accepted the news without further comment. Once again, Pirie saw the unpredictable moodiness of the girl, the sudden shifts of disposition and energies.

"Why don't you get your guitar and we'll play together," Pirie suggested and saw Peely break into a happy smile.

"That'd be fun," she laughed. "We haven't played together in a long, long time."

Two years, to be exact, Pirie added silently as Peely rushed off to get her instrument. Pirie got her own guitar and both girls went outside to sit under the big Acacia. Pirie's intent was to stay close to Peely till she had to meet Doc Gallagher. She wanted no incidents to possibly interfere with the Doctor's visit and so the hours passed quickly as the two sisters sang and strummed and talked of good times past. They made a lunch of lettuce and potato salad and then returned to their instruments. In mid-afternoon Peely's energy gave out and Pirie was happy it had lasted that long. As she watched her sister go to sleep quickly in her room, she closed the door, glanced at her watch and saw it was nearly four o'clock. She'd start for her meeting with Doctor Gallagher at the main fork in the road outside Grandview.

As she drove along the bayou road, she shuddered as the night before came upon her. The slow water was merely placid and almost inviting now, the vines hanging limply, the leaves only leaves. How very different they seemed. It made her wonder about the powers of the mind. Death stalked her here at Moonwater, but not just death. There was something more, something beyond the terror of death, something which, if she managed to elude the hand of death, would remain with her forever. She knew that much now, knew it not by reason but by a strange inner knowledge that was as yet unsorted, undissected, and yes, unwanted. But it was there. She shuddered again and was glad to see the road open up beyond the bayous to the flat country. When this was over and done with she would never return to Moonwater, she promised herself and at once, with frightening immediacy, the thought leaped into her mind, a mocking answer; perhaps she would never leave Moonwater alive. Once more she shook away her thoughts and slowed as the fork in the road came up before her. She pulled over to the shoulder of the road and waited to see Doctor Gallagher driving out from the road to Grandview.

She settled back against the seat, resting her head back. She was probably a little early, she realized. A big produce truck came lumbering down the road and turned off at the right fork that led to the next county. Two cars did the same. Most traffic turned either right or left at the fork, for very few people had reason to go into the bayou country, even so far as Moonwater. Even less ventured beyond into the back lands. More cars and a bus came and turned and Pirie glanced at her watch. Doctor Gallagher could easily have been detained. He would have had a full day, she knew. She observed the minute hand move around the face of her watch. Waiting was always such an impatient chore. A schoolbus came down the road from the opposite direction and turned onto the road to Grandview. More cars passed and an uneasy apprehension was gripping her. He should have been here by now. She put the car into gear and drove down the road toward Grandview, driving slowly. There weren't that many cars on the road and she'd have to meet him on the way, so at every oncoming car she braked and peered at the driver, only to move on, her lips setting a little tighter each time. Finally she was at Grandview and she drove down Catalpa toward Doctor Gallagher's office. As she pulled up in front of the low, brick building she was relieved to see the lone light on inside his office window. He had been delayed, she murmured, letting her breath escape with a great whooshing sound. Probably he'd tried to call her but she had already left.

She went up the few steps to the door and opened it. There was no one in the small waiting room and the door to the inner office was ajar.

"Doctor Gallagher?" she called. "It's me, Pirie."

There was no answer and a sudden stab of fright went through her. She called again and still there was no answer.

She pushed open the door and stood still, trying to find a scream that wouldn't come, her flesh crawling, tingling, her heart pounding against her ribs. Dr. Gallagher was at his desk, slumped over it, an ugly, sickening stream of red coming from his temple. In his right hand he held a revolver, his lifeless fingers still curled around the trigger.

Pirie grasped the edge of the door to steady herself as she saw the room sway. She pressed her eyes tightly shut and then opened them again and the room stopped swaying. But her heart continued to crash wildly against her ribs as countless jumbled emotions ran wild through her body, Shock, fear, pity, pain, consternation, all of these ran through her mind and one more, one strange and perhaps selfish feeling. She felt cheated, as though a promise had been broken, a door slammed shut in her face. She had pinned all her hopes on Doctor Gallagher and she almost heard herself telling the still form that he had no right to do this, no right to leave Peely and her with no place to turn. She moved forward into the room and forced herself to reach across the desk to the telephone at the man's elbow. With hardly seeing eyes she noticed there was some kind of a note lying half-under his head and she pulled her eyes away to dial Sheriff Whittaker. She heard her own voice, a dull monotone, as the Sheriff answered.

"This is Pirie DuChamps," she said. "I just came in to Doctor Gallagher's office. He's dead. He shot himself. Please come over right away."

She put down the phone, hearing only the Sheriff's gasp of shock, and then she walked to a corner of the room and stood there, wanting not to look at the figure slumped over the desk, yet unable to look anywhere else. The Sheriff's office was fairly close by and yet it seemed an hour before he arrived, rushing in with a deputy behind him. He had his assistant, a young officer she didn't know, sit her on the couch and give her a small white tablet with a cup of water. "Mild tranquilizer, Miss," the young officer said. "We've seen people suddenly go to pieces afterwards."

She thanked him but she knew she'd have no hysterics. She felt too completely dead inside for that. She wanted to think about Doctor Gallagher, and why he'd done such a terrible thing to himself, and to feel pain for him. But all she could think about was returning to Moonwater, returning alone, defeated, her hopes turned to ashes. And death waiting there to try again. Dimly, she heard herself vowing to flee, to take Peely and flee. She didn't know where or how but it was all that was left. Sheriff Whitaker's voice brought her attention back to the room.

"I don't want to touch a thing until Bert gets here," the Sheriff said. "After he's through taking pictures we can start to work. But he left a note, I can read it over his shoulder. 'Friends, there is no way for me to explain and so I shall waste no time trying to do so. It had to be and that is enough.' "

The Sheriff stepped back and pursed his lips. "It sure beats me," he said to no one in particular. "I guess I'm getting too old to figure out things like this anymore."

The door opened and Pirie saw Bert Fromm come in. She and Bert had graduated from Grandview High together. He was the school photographer then and she'd heard he'd gone on to open up his own studio and had become practically the whole town's official photographer. She watched him go to work quickly, professionally, taking pictures of the desk and the body from every angle. She got up and stood behind him as he photographed the desk from in back of Doctor Gallagher's body and she let her eyes see the view as his camera would record it; the body fallen down onto the desk, the gun held in his right hand, his head partially on the sheet of paper with the note written on it, the pen beside the paper. It was a scene that would stay etched in her mind forever, she knew, and as she turned away she felt herself frowning. Some thing was wrong about that scene. She looked again and she couldn't be sure but something was wrong. She let her eyes stay riveted on the grisly scene, forcing herself to take in every little detail and as her frown deepened, she felt her heart start to pound again. Was she being stupid, silly, overimaginative? Was she seeing shadows where there were no shadows? Was she trying to bend little things to make them into bigger things, letting her own fears distort reality? She wanted more time to think about what she'd seen. She wouldn't say anything now and be rebuffed or seem a foolish, over-wrought female.

Bert Fromm had finished his work and she went up to him. He gave her a sympathetic smile at once. "Too bad you had to walk in on him, Pirie," Bert said. "Rough, I imagine."

She nodded. "When will you develop the pictures you took, Bert?" she asked.

"Right away," he answered. "I'm going back to my studio and have prints for the Sheriff in about fifteen minutes. That's regulations for Police work, fast prints."

"May I come with you," Pirie asked. "I want a print of that shot you took of the desk."

She saw Bert's eyebrows go up and the strange expression creep into his eyes.

"I know," she said quickly. "It sounds awfully macabre and ghoulish but it's not anything like that. Just believe me, it isn't. I want to study something and I can't talk about it now, not till I'm more sure myself."

Bert shrugged and took her arm.

"For you, Pirie, it's a deal," he said. "Come on, let's get out of here."

CHAPTER SEVEN

Bert's studio was a half dozen blocks away—a neat, professional place with negatives and prints hanging from clips attached to wires like some abstracts, close up modern design. Lights and camera equipment lined the walls and Pirie found herself stepping over dozens of cables and wires on the floor. Pushing aside a sheaf of photos, he found a spot for her at the edge of a leather couch.

"Stay put and I'll be out of the darkroom in about ten minutes," he said. "I'd take you in with me but I work better and faster alone."

Pirie nodded, grateful for the chance to put her head back and be alone with her thoughts. Bert disappeared into the darkroom and she saw the little red bulb go on outside the door. She glanced at her watch and bit her lower lip. She shouldn't have left Peely this long and she wondered if she should just steal away and rush back to Moonwater. But she didn't. She wanted that print, wanted to study it again, to see if the picture itself would scream out at her and tell her she'd been right. She closed her eyes and waited, opening them only when she heard the door opening and Bert coming out, turning a dozen prints in his hand.

"There you are, Pirie," he said, handing her one. She took it soundlessly, her eyes searching it, and the thing she had noted was there, leaping out at her. Bert handed her a manila envelope and she slipped the print inside.

"Thank you, Bert," she said, her eyes wide, grave. She saw Bert studying her, wondering about her. "I'll be in touch," she said, opening the door.

"Do that," Bert answered. "I'd be interested."

Pirie walked out into the night street of the town, the envelope with the photo inside it clutched to her breast, a picture that said so much, so terrifyingly much. But did it only say it to her, she wondered again. The thought of it dazed her, overwhelmed her, and once again she had the feeling of doors slammed in her face, of being cornered by an evil which was closing every avenue of escape. She passed Sheriff Whittaker's office and wondered if she shouldn't go inside and wait there for him to return. But she recalled his answer when she had told him about the bridge over Thompson's marsh. He'd said she had been "plumb lucky" when crossing it that first time and she knew that Sheriff Whittaker was no one to turn to with the photo she clutched in her hands. She had never realized how much evil depends on the unwitting help of literal, unimaginative people. Was there no one who might be able to see as she saw? She thought of Byron Lee and felt the temptation to call him. But Byron was not above suspicion. Not that she really suspected Byron—yet she had promised herself to stick with logic and logic had to include Byron. Logic, she snorted grimly, logic where there was no place for logic, where strange forces gave the lie to reason and logic, where the unexplainable ruled. In horror she had to face that which she already knew deep down inside her: that there was no place to turn.

"Pirie." The voice, calling her name in the dark, startled her and she jumped. The figure, large and moving quickly, came toward her.

"Adam," she exclaimed, the relief in her voice unmistakable. Adam Bailey's eyes were studying her drawn face, she saw, and there was more concern than curiosity in them. It was good to see concern, a quality she hadn't seen in a long time.

"You look like you've seen a dead man," Adam said. "What's the matter?"

"That was a good choice then," Pirie said, "I have. Doctor Gallagher."

Quickly, hearing herself stammer in haste, she told Adam Bailey of finding Doctor Gallagher and she felt his arm take hers, his strength a warming, comforting thing to feel.

"Come on up to my office," he said. "I want to hear more about this. But you need something, first."

He led her, unprotesting, around the corner and into the doorway of the neat, white building, one of the newer ones in Grandview. His office, lined with law books and old English hunting prints, was a reassuring, comfortable place, very much like Adam Bailey, she decided quickly. She sank into the deep leather chair where he placed her and watched him go to a wooden cabinet in the wall. He took out an electric coffee maker and cups and plugged in the machine. While the coffee perked, he brought out a bottle of brandy and poured some into a snifter.

"Drink this, first," he said, watching her intently. Happy to have someone concerned over her, she sipped the brandy and felt its warmth rush down inside her, spreading out to paint her insides with a tingly reviving substance. She finished the brandy and then found the coffee waiting for her. Adam had a cup of it with her.

"Some of what you said before didn't make too much sense," he said, but not unkindly. "Suppose you start again and let me have it more slowly. Start with that letter you said Peely sent you."

Pirie began again and told him every little detail she could remember, hearing her words rushing out of her as if she were another person, somehow detached, listening on the side. Adam listened intently, only interrupting her twice to have her rethink an incident. She was more than halfway through before she realized he had been making small notes on a slip of paper as she talked. She ended her story back in Doctor Gallagher's office as she'd looked over Bert Fromm's shoulder while he took his pictures.

"And you say you don't believe Doctor Gallagher took his own life," Adam commented. "Why don't you believe it?"

She bit her lips and opened the envelope. She had blurted out everything else, all the things she knew but couldn't prove. One more now wouldn't hurt. She handed the young lawyer the photo, watched him open the envelope and study it.

"I confess I don't see anything that startles me," Adam Bailey said. "But I don't know what I'm supposed to be looking for."

"Do you see the pen beside the note paper?" Pirie asked.

"Yes," Adam said, "just to the left of it." Pirie nodded, her eyes grave.

"Exactly," she said. "To the left of it. Doctor Gallagher wasn't left-handed, Adam. He, and any right-handed person, would have put the pen down at the right of the note."

She watched Adam Bailey's frown start to spread across his forehead as he looked at the photo again, peering intently at it. Then he glanced up at Pirie, his eyes narrowed.

"Very observant," he commented. "It's a little thing, but it could be meaningful, especially if it's connected with something more. And there is something more, isn't there?"

Pirie nodded again. "Valonia is left-handed," she said, almost choking on the words. But then she was happy to have given voice to the thought. It had seized her and held her in fear and horror and now it was freed. Adam Bailey sat back in the chair behind his desk, looking from the photo to Pirie and back again.

"I know, it doesn't prove anything," she said dejectedly and met his steady gaze. "That's why I didn't say anything to Sheriff Whittaker. I guess you don't believe me, either."

"You're right, it doesn't prove anything," Adam said and Pirie noted the fact that he hadn't taken up her last statement one way or the other. "The pen could have rolled over to the left side of the note when his hand fell forward after he shot himself," the lawyer added. Pirie felt her spirits sinking faster. That was more or less what Sheriff Whittaker would have said. She got up quickly, afraid the torrent of tears edging her eyes would burst forth.

"I'm sorry I've been such a bother," she said and ran for the door. Adam Bailey moved fast and was holding her arm as she reached the doorknob, pulling her back and now the tears were flowing down her cheeks.

"Hold on, there," he said and through a watery curtain she thought she saw him smile as he guided her back to the leather chair. "I didn't say I didn't believe you," he said, handing her a nice large man-sized handkerchief. She forced herself to stop sniffling. She absolutely deplored sniffling girls.

"Calm down," he said sternly. "I want to hear everything you've said to me over again, from the very beginning."

He sat back and she went through it all again, this time ending up with her shock at seeing the pen at the left side of the note. Once more Adam Bailey's face was noncommittal and she knew he still hadn't really said he believed her.

"You think this woman, Valonia, killed Doctor Gallagher and faked it as a suicide," he said, thinking aloud, looking off at one of the wall prints. "But wasn't she at the house with you and Peely all afternoon, until you left to meet Doctor Gallagher? When could she have come into town to do this?"

"I don't know that she was at Moonwater," Pirie said. "I thought about that earlier and realized that Peely and I never did see her all day. We were having so much fun together we paid no attention to anything else. Valonia could have left the back way anytime and I wouldn't have known it."

"I see," Adam said. "So that much is possible. But why wasn't the shot heard? It had to be done sometime between four and five and certainly there are lots of people on the streets passing by at that time."

"Doctor Gallagher's inside offices were soundproof," Pirie said. "I remember my mother telling me about them when I was little. Doc Gallagher had a lot of little ones to give injections to regularly and you know the way most kids scream even at the sight of a needle. He didn't want his patients in the waiting room hearing their high-pitched wails, so he purposely had the inner offices soundproofed."

Adam Bailey's eyes were narrowed, a hardness in them she'd never seen there before. "Most interesting," he said. "If your suspicions are true, there are even more unusual elements at work here than in an ordinary murder case—things beyond our comprehension to fully understand."

Pirie looked at Adam Bailey's no-nonsense, rugged countenance, at the young lawyer's stern eyes.

"Don't tell me you believe in kas and astral doubles," she asked incredulously and Adam smiled.

"I don't know that I believe in anything like that," he said. "But I believe that there are many things we neither understand nor comprehend about the nature of man and his own powers. However, that's not my main concern, not yet, anyway."

Adam got up and came over to the leather chair and gazed sternly into the girl's eyes.

"You are my main concern," he said slowly, evenly, spacing out each word. "You can't go on in this alone. I'm surprised you haven't gone screaming off somewhere before this. You're quite a remarkable girl, Pirie Du-Champs."

Pirie managed a smile she found someplace down deep inside her. "And you're a great guy for not having laughed at me," she said.

"Look, I'll be honest with you, Pirie," Adam said, straightening up. "Nothing you said could stand up in a court of law, not even in a pre-trial examination. But I believe you and I'm going to help you."

She wanted to reach up and throw her arms around him but she somehow found the strength to hold back. But she could not hold back the question which fell from her tongue. "Why do you believe me, Adam?"

Adam smiled at her. "There are no deep, hidden reasons," he said. "I don't think you could make up all these wild things you've been telling. And I don't see any reason for you to do so. That and the fact that Peely is definitely ill. Something, I'm not sure what yet, but something is very wrong at Moonwater."

"Amen," Pirie breathed and closed her eyes, hardly able to believe she had found another door, a place to turn.

"But we've got to get facts, Pirie, evidence, proof," Adam said. "And we can't do it by taking the time for the killer or killers to strike again."

"I thought of running off with Peely," Pirie said.

"Maybe. It might be necessary as a protective measure. But running is never much of an answer for anything. I thought about your not returning to Moonwater but that's no good, either. It might trigger the killers into something more desperate. Right now you're going to have to go back, but I'll drive out tomorrow and see you. I want the night to think about what we can do and how to do it."

"Yes, I've got to go back," the girl echoed. "I've left Peely alone too long now. Remember, I told you how I even wondered about Peely and the bridge? Well, Doctor Gallagher's murder proves Peely's innocent. Whoever tampered with the bridge murdered Doc Gallagher and that couldn't have been Peely."

"If Doc Gallagher was murdered," Adam said and Pirie halted in surprise. "Until we can prove otherwise—it's suicide." His face was stern but his eyes were soft and understanding and suddenly she couldn't help herself and she found her arms around his neck, her lips brushing his. He had that warm, cozy odor of tweed and pipe tobacco about him.

"Thank you, Adam," she said simply. "Thank you so very much." His lips, even for the brief instant, were strong and warm and then she pulled away, embarrassed, to see him grinning down at her.

"I don't usually get my fee so far in advance," he said. She didn't dare voice any of the half dozen answers that flew to her tongue. Instead, she turned and hurried from the office to where she'd left the little old car near Doctor Gallagher's and at the sight of the Doctor's office a terrible rage exploded inside her. They would pay for this, she promised herself, they would pay for it. Whoever it was, she added, mindful of Adam's words about proof. But she knew full well who "they" were. As she drove home, sending the car speeding around the dark roads of the bayou land, making herself look straight ahead and ignoring the twisted black night forms outside, she thought of Byron Lee and felt guilty. She had suspected Peely and had found how wrong she'd been and she was confident her suspicions about Byron Lee would be just as unfounded. Still, he had been terribly upset when she refused to agree to get Peely to sell Moonwater. With Peely outside suspicion now, only Byron, Valonia and Barlow were left. And of the three, she still had no clear motives for Valonia and Barlow. But she would find them, she vowed as she turned into the driveway of the big, "beautifully ugly" house.

Valonia opened the door and Robert Barlow stood just in back of her. Pirie tried to read the woman's impassive face but it said nothing.

"We heard about Doctor Gallagher," Robert Barlow said. "There was an announcement on the radio just now. I'm sure it was a terrible shock for you, my dear."

"Yes," the girl replied. "But then I'm getting used to shocks."

"I had hoped your talk with Doc Asher would have convinced you we are doing the right thing for Peely," Barlow said. "But apparently it didn't because you went ahead with your plans to have her see Gallagher. Perhaps now you'll stop this uncooperative, ungrateful behavior. Doctor Gallagher's suicide was a sign that you were not to see him. Let it be a lesson to you."

Threats thinly concealed? Pirie pondered the question as her eyes met Barlow's arrogant stare. She looked away at Valonia and the woman's burning eyes glittered.

"We called Doc Asher about Peely's increasing tendency to wander and run away," Valonia said. "On his advice I have moved my bed into Peely's room. I will sleep there at night. That way I will hear her if she tries to go out."

Pirie heard her own breath draw in sharply. They were getting more clever. This maneuver put an end to any plans she might have had to sneak away in the night with Peely. Had they envisioned such a move as a logical possibility? Or had they some other way of anticipating her thoughts?

"I think I should be the one to sleep in with Peely," Pirie said, trying to counter this latest ploy.

"You'll have to discuss that with Doc Asher," Robert Barlow said. "We're acting strictly on his advice in this area."

Pirie grimaced inwardly. Neat, she admitted bitterly to herself. They had tossed the ball to the back country fraud who would, of course, field it equally cleverly if she confronted him with her demand. Turning on her heel, she went upstairs, stopping first at Peely's room. Peely brightened at seeing her, clothed in light blue pajamas and sitting atop the bed with a book. But the girl never asked what had happened to Doctor Gallagher's visit. She seemed to have quite forgotten about it and Pirie saw her eyes wander aimlessly, vacantly, as they talked. She felt herself torn between pity and helpless fury. Against the right wall of the room she saw Valonia's bed, an old-fashioned iron-framed one, with a long, heavy nightgown resting over the rear frame. Valonia's own room was on the third floor, just above Peely's, and had belonged to the previous housekeeper. As she thought about it, Pirie realized she had not been in that room since Valonia had come to Moonwater. She heard the rustling sound of Valonia's long dress in the hall outside and the door opened to admit the big woman.

"I'll see you in the morning, hon," Pirie said to her sister and went out at once. In her own room she locked the door and undressed, the events of the last few hours sweeping over her like a blanket of smothering, oppressive memories and she felt suddenly exhausted, completely drained of energy. In the darkness, the warm air carrying the honeysuckle sweetness into the room, she let herself think of her meeting with Adam Bailey and she drew comfort from the vision of his strong face as he listened to her tell her story. It all came back to her as she thought about it and again she realized how many elements "beyond our comprehension to fully understand" were part of all this terror and killing. Peely's illness, for one thing. It was somehow connected. And Peely's shockingly accurate vision of that dress, that was somehow connected, too. It was strange how tonight she was less fearful for her own safety, yet there had been no lessening of the silent danger—the sudden, unexpected hand of death. But the reason for that was her meeting with Adam, she realized. Dear God, let nothing happen to him, she silently prayed in the darkness of the room. There was so much unfinished. There were murderers to catch, not just for her sake, nor for Peely's, but for Doc Gallagher's. If she hadn't insisted on his seeing Peely the man would still be alive, Pirie told herself, and she felt the hard-steel core of determination grow inside her. There would be no running away, not for her, she knew. Not until she had the answers to the unanswered, explanations for the unexplained. She closed her eyes finally and let the exhaustion of her body and spirit push her into sleep.

CHAPTER EIGHT

W as there a new boldness to Valonia and Barlow, Pirie won- dered in the morning? Or was it her imagination being overactive again? The woman's comments had a sharpness to them, her tone a new note of authority. It was quickly made plain when Pirie spoke of going into Grandview with Peely.

"Peely's to go nowhere without Doc Asher's permission," Valonia said, staring down at Pirie. The girl felt the anger in her own eyes flash as, fighting down the impulse to cringe before the big woman's gaunt, demoniacal presence, she held her gaze steady.

"I don't need his permission to take Peely into town or any- where else," Pirie snapped and at once she heard Robert Barlow's smooth, deep voice. He had come silently into the room.

"Of course not, my dear," he said. "It's just that Valonia is upset over Peely's condition, just as you are. We're all upset. It's been a trying time. But Doc Asher is stopping by this morning to see Peely and to bring some more medicine. He ought to be here any minute."

Pirie, tight-lipped, turned and walked out of the house. There was nothing she could do yet but stand by helplessly. She couldn't even muster a logical, reasonable objection to Doc Asher's visit. Not without support, the kind of support she had felt certain to get from Doctor Gallagher. She saw the trees move at the open- ing beyond the house where the road to the back country began and the small rig came slowly through, Doc Asher's lean figure holding the reins.

"Good morning," he said brightly as he hopped down, a fast smile vanishing as quickly as it had appeared. He strode past Pirie and into the house. The girl decided to stay outside. There was nothing to be gained by going in except more bitter words and words were meaningless now. Only actions would help—proof, evidence, as Adam had said.

The doctor's visit was brief and as he came out, Pirie blocked the path. "I understand you ordered Valonia to sleep in with Peely," she said. "Frankly, I think I should be the one to do that."

The small man smiled again and his intense blue eyes moved disconcertingly as he spoke.

"Ordinarily you would be right, my dear," he said. "But in these particular circumstances I do not feel your affirmations are correct for your sister."

Pirie heard her temper snap. "Just what the hell does that mean?" she exploded. Unfazed, Doc Asher tossed off another quick smile.

"Affirmations are those forces of thought which can be directed toward a specific goal. They also help a person accept conditions he or she may be unable to change. A person with sympathetic affirmations will be good for your sister. Yours, however, would create an even greater disturbance in her condition."

With a last little smile, almost apologetic, he moved on and climbed into the rig. Pirie watched him go. He had, as she had expected, neatly turned aside her query. There was no doubt any longer that he was working hand in hand with Barlow and Valonia. She would have scoffed at his psychic mumbojumbo a few days ago. It was with a sense of shock that she realized she was no longer sure where the real and the unreal parted company. Or if they ever really did.

Peely came out to interrupt her thoughts, a small basket in her hand. She wanted to gather some wildflowers for the dinner table and Pirie went with her. They walked into the cool shade of the great cypresses and down to the edge of the bayous, almost to the very spot where the log had hurtled out of the night at Pirie. Peely gathered a dozen swamp lilies and when they returned to Moonwater, Pirie saw the unfamiliar cream colored car there. When Adam unfolded himself from the front seat her heart soared. Peely went on into the house as Adam embraced Pirie with a wide smile.

"Valonia told me you were out flower-gathering," he said, taking the girl's arm. Casually, smoothly, he steered her far enough from the house so they could talk without being overheard. His easy, calm, almost bland manner did wonders for the girl's turbulent heart.

"We'll walk around and you make like you're showing me the place," he said. "I did a lot of thinking last night and so far I haven't come up with very much. I need a bottle of that medicine they've been giving Peely. I want to have it analyzed at the hospital lab in Cotile. Do you think you can get it for me?"

"I'll get it," Pirie answered grimly.

"Good girl," Adam said as they rounded a corner of the house, walking slowly, casually. "The next item could be called an operating rule. You are not to go anywhere without letting me know where you're going and when. You have my office number. I have an answering service and if I'm not there when you call I'll check in soon after and get your message."

She felt herself grow all warm inside and filled with the security of their conspiratorial confidences. They were passing the remnants of the little garden when Adam halted and knelt down beside the bed of plants with the creamy white flowers.

"Mandrake," he commented softly.

"Yes," Pirie said in some surprise. "That's what Valonia said they were called."

"Did she plant them?" Adam asked, running his fingers down the green stem of one of the plants.

"She said they just grew there," Pirie replied. "But they weren't there when I left two years ago."

Pirie heard the sound of the side door opening and looked up to see Valonia standing there. Adam, kneeling beside the plants, gave the big, gaunt woman a wide smile. Valonia's face remained carved in stone.

"Interesting plants, these Mandrakes," he said, looking up at Pirie. "Legend has it that the Mandrake is a resting place for certain malevolent spirits. At certain times, when a Mandrake root is pulled from the ground, a humanoid cry is supposed to be heard, the cry being that of the spirit in the roots."

"How in heavens did a tale like that ever get started?" Pirie frowned. Adam Bailey shrugged and smiled up at Valonia again.

"How did any of the ancient legends and superstitions get started?" he said. "Actually, if the plant is pulled up wholly by the root there sometimes is a pulling, sucking sound that could be interpreted as a kind of soft cry. But the Mandrake itself has been used by the ancient Egyptians and the Romans as an anesthetic. The old Germanic tribes used it as an aid to conception and it's used in many parts of the world today as herb medicine. In some places the plant is known as Devil's apples."

"I'm impressed," Pirie said as Adam stood up. "How do you know so much about botany?"

"I've always been interested in it," he answered, taking Pirie's arm and walking on with her. "I might have become a botanist if law hadn't called more strongly to me."

Pirie felt Valonia's eyes burning into her back as they walked on and Adam steered her across the lawn to where his car stood. He opened the door and she sat inside as he slipped behind the wheel.

"Before I go, I want to hear again about that near accident you had coming down here from New York," he said. "I want every little detail you can remember."

Pirie went over it again and when she was finished Adam questioned her in lawyer-like fashion, making sure he had certain points firmly in his mind.

"The big route sign with the number nine flashed in front of your eyes a second before the lights dazzled you?" he queried and she nodded. "And the brooch you were wearing, the amulet, had nine small stones around the center stone?" Again Pirie nodded. "And it's opal, right?" he concluded.

"Right," she said. "But you're not seriously trying to connect that freak accident with anything that's happened here, are you, Adam?"

"I'm not trying to connect anything," he answered, giving her a broad grin. "I'm just interested in everything."

His hand was on hers suddenly, squeezing her fingers together in a gesture of reassurance. She had the real desire to cling to his rugged frame, to thank him again with her lips, but this time she held back. She was in no emotional state to properly sort out her feelings. What she felt for Adam might be only an overwhelming sense of gratitude for his comforting presence or perhaps only her own female need for. a moment's tender concern.

"I'll come back tomorrow evening," he said. "Get that bottle of Asher's medicine but don't do anything foolish."

She nodded but held her fingers crossed behind her back. She knew that she'd do almost anything to get that bottle. It could hold the answers to a lot of questions. Adam's hand on her cheek was gentle and warm and then she swung out of the car. "Tomorrow evening," she said. "I'll be waiting."

He waved and drove away and she was alone again but not really, not like before. A sudden wind whipped at her and she look skyward to see gray clouds scudding across the old house. More grayness came on their heels and she felt the wind again. A storm was coming on fast and she went inside and up to her room. The rain started to come down within the hour, a hard, driving rain, and the wind with it made the old house groan and creak in protest. Peely came into her room and they watched the rain trace wind-swept patterns of wetness on the windows. Peely seemed strangely stimulated by the storm, watching the bending trees in animation and excitement, following the sweep of the wind with her eyes. With every blast that struck hard at the old house, making it shudder, the girl clasped her arms together and laughed softly. Pirie could think only of Emerson's words as Peely seemed "enclosed in a tumultuous privacy of storm," finding some secret bond with the storm outside and her own inner turmoil.

The hard, driving rain lasted through the day and ended after dinner and, almost at once, as though refreshed and renewed, the honeysuckle and mimosa took over the land with their heavy, sweet scents. Scattered clusters of rain still held by the trees continued to splatter against the house and in the distance thunder rumbled.

"Sounds like another storm might be on its way," Robert Barlow commented during dessert and Pirie smiled sweetly back at him. Dinner had been a largely silent affair but the girl, determined to play the game in return, matched Barlow's bland comments with equally contained coolness. If only he knew how her insides were jumping, she murmured silently. Valonia served as usual but without a word and Pirie did her best to ignore the woman. When dinner was finished, Pirie saw her sister back to her room where, like the storm that had gone, Peely lay silent and spent. Pirie took the moment to search through the girl's dresser, hoping a bottle of the medicine might be there. But there was none and it had been only a wild hope anyway. She didn't really expect Valonia to be that careless. She slammed the bottom drawer shut as she heard the rustling sounds of the woman's long gray dress coming down the hall. Seated on the bed beside Peely when Valonia entered the room, Pirie looked up casually to meet the woman's burning, piercing eyes, eyes that seemed to look right through her—and Pirie wondered if they did. She kissed Peely good night and left.

She didn't fear for the girl's safety at the woman's hands. They were too clever to do anything direct. It was the subtle, the indirect that she had to guard against. But tonight she had some very direct plans of her own. Having Valonia spend the nights in Peely's room had been aimed at her, she knew. But they had outwitted themselves, she smiled grimly. This gave her a clear opportunity she might never have had otherwise to go into Valonia's room and get the medicine. Pirie put on her oldest blue jeans and a dark blue shirt. Turning off her lights, she lay down on the bed to wait for the night to lengthen.

Lying awake in the darkened room, she felt her senses heighten, become more aware of every little sound. She heard Valonia's long dress rustle down the hall once, twice and then she heard Barlow's voice. She lay still, listening, and heard the woman return and the faint click of Peely's door being closed at the far end of the hall. She continued to lay still until she heard the sound of another door closing downstairs. That would be Barlow, she told herself, using the master bedroom at the rear of the ground floor. The night sent a probing finger of wind into the room and she listened to the menacing rumble of thunder, growing louder now. Her window was lighted for an instant with the blue flare of lighting and the thunder cascaded behind it. Outside the trees shook in unison as a gust of wind swept through them. Pirie forced herself to stay there, on the bed. She wanted to give everyone ample time to fall asleep.

It was just past midnight, with the coming storm still hovering nearby, that she rose from the bed and took a small flashlight from inside her suitcase. Tying a hair ribbon to the end of it she hung it around her neck and slowly, carefully, eased the door of the room open. The hall was black and the only sound was the steady rumble of the thunder. She closed the door, holding the knob so the latch wouldn't snap back with a noise, and then edged her way to the stairs. She walked barefoot, taking each step by testing it first, all too aware of the creaking boards of the old house. Midway up the stairs she paused to listen but all was still inside the house. Wiping her wet palms on her trousers she continued climbing the steps to the top floor of the house, moving along the edge of the balcony where the boards were least apt to sag and creak.

Valonia's room was the one at the far end of the third floor hall and she moved toward it with her back against the wall, taking small steps, grateful for the thickness of the floors of the old house. As she passed one of the hall windows a flash of lightning turned night into fleeting day and she saw the closed door of the room just ahead of her. She took the doorknob in her hand and turned, taking care again not to let the latch snap. But the knob moved only half a turn. The door was locked. She leaned her shoulder against it and pressed but the stout wooden door wouldn't give a fraction of an inch.

Dammit! Pirie swore silently. It just hadn't occurred to her that the room would be locked. But she wasn't giving up. Another chance like this might never come. There was another door to the left, a room which adjoined Valonia's and Pirie called upon her memory to supply the details. It had been part of the housekeeper's living quarters but then it had been used as a kind of storeroom for odds and ends. She turned the knob and the door opened. She was inside the room.

Another flash of lightning considerately illuminated the room long enough for her to see a jumble of boxes and cartons, an old spinning wheel, tables piled on top of one another and a general clutter of odd pieces of furniture. But the door to Valonia's room was unobstructed and she hurried over to it, bumping her hip against the corner of a table in the darkness that followed the brief flash of light. She turned the knob and swore again. It, too, was locked. The room lit up once more as a blue flash from outside tore through the night and Pirie saw the window at the end of the room. She made her way to it, squeezing through the cartons and tables and general clutter. The window opened as she raised it slowly, ever so slowly to avoid scrapes and creaks. Outside, the shingles of the sloping side of the roof led down to a narrow rain gutter of copper. Valonia's room with its two windows looked out parallel about fifteen feet away.

Pirie climbed out the window, putting one leg out first, her foot groping along the shingles, trying to find a spot it could grip. A broken shingle furnished just enough of a hold and she pulled the rest of her body onto the sloping edge of the roof, hanging onto the window sill with her hands. Slowly, she began to lower herself down toward the narrow rain gutter, feeling with her feet as she clung to the window sill. Her arms were stretched out as far as they could go and she still hadn't made contact with the gutter drain. With a short prayer she let go of the window sill and pressed herself tight against the shingles, clawing at them with her hands as she felt her body slide down the slope of the roof. And then her feet touched the rain gutter, cold and wet against her skin. But she had stopped sliding and she stayed there for a long moment getting her breath. The window was above her, out of reach. She wouldn't be returning through it, she knew. But she'd think about that problem later. She had already learned that one step at a time was all she could handle.

Keeping her body pressed tightly against the sloped roof line, she moved carefully along the copper drain, testing each step with her bare feet. The fifteen feet seemed like fifty and she paused for breath every few feet. She had to stay tight against the roof line or lose her balance and fall. But finally she was at the first window of Valonia's room and stretching up, she could just get her fingers onto the sill. She was grateful for the fact that the gables of the old house were at different levels and she could reach the window.

Pulling with her finger tips and pushing with her legs against the roof, she managed to get a hand onto the sill and finally an arm and she clung there, catching her breath. Pushing up against the window, she was relieved to see it rise. Getting her head through a space, she used her shoulders to push the window up higher and pulled herself into the room. The lightning flashed behind her and the thunder grew louder. The storm was no longer hovering in the distance but coming on fast. Pirie took the flashlight from around her neck and shone it into the room. The one wall was bare, empty, where Valonia's bed had stood. A row of books lined the top of an old dresser and she went over to them. *Ectenic Forces,* she read on the binding of the first thick volume. A thinner one followed: *Diagrams and Their Use.* Pirie made a mental note of the titles as she scanned the books. *Ritual use of Herbs and Roots* was another. A particularly thick volume was entitled *The Kabbalah and Theomancy.*

There were more, many more, but Pirie turned her attention to the rest of the room, searching for what she had come for. a small private bath was to the left and she hurried into it, the small beam of the flashlight being assisted by periodic bursts of lightning. Inside the medicine cabinet, on the lower shelf, she saw six unmarked, filled bottles. She put down her light and opened one. The terribly acrid, bitter odor assailed her nostrils at once and she immediately knew it was the bottle she sought. She closed the cabinet and started out of the bathroom and she heard the sound in the hallway, a rustling, swishing sound. Her heart froze. She heard the sound of keys being taken out of a pocket just outside the door and on silent bare feet she raced across the room to the door to the adjoining storeroom. But it was locked from the inside, too.

The sound of a key being put into the door galvanized her into frantic speed. Stuffing the bottle into her bra, she clambered out the window and went sliding and slipping down the shingles, managing to arrest her fall against the rain gutter. Desperation lending strength and recklessness to her, Pirie clambered to the side of the gable and pressed herself flat against it. The gable was not a high one but the triangular side would hide her if she could hold there long enough. A flash of lightning illumined the girl's slender figure, plastered against the slope of the roof, wedged into the crack where the gable met the roof line like some giant fly. Pirie heard the window being raised higher and she knew Valonia was peering out, her piercing eyes searching the roof, the line of the drain. A loud clap of thunder exploded and let loose a torrent of rain. Pirie felt the shingles grow wet and she dug her heels into the slope of the roof but she was beginning to slide. Desperately, she pressed her elbows back into the wood until she could press no more. But in seconds the torrent of rain had drenched her and turned her into a wet, slippery object and she felt her legs going out from under her as she slid down. She heard the window bang shut just as she slipped below the line of the gable to come to rest against the copper drain. Holding her breath, illuminated again by a flash of lightning, the girl waited for death. If Valonia had seen her, all the woman would need to do would be to lean out the window and push and Pirie would go hurtling from the roof.

But she had been lucky. The woman had slammed the window shut and turned away at once, just as the girl slid into view. Pirie stayed quiet, waiting for her legs to stop trembling. The rain slammed into her and coursed along the copper drain gutter, swishing over her feet and turning the already precarious hold into a wet, slippery tightrope. Death could seize her at any moment, she knew. It didn't need Valonia's helping hand. What had made the woman come up to her room, the girl wondered. What had made the woman waken in the dead of night and investigate her room? No noise had wakened her, Pirie was certain of that. She knew it was but one more unexplainable occurrence to add to the strange and frightening list.

But her legs had stopped trembling enough to try and move and she edged her way along the drain, clinging at each flash of lightning. There was no way to reach the window from which she'd first dropped onto the roof, so she moved forward in the opposite direction, trying to recall the plan of the top floor of the house. A window in the hall looked out directly at the end of the hall, which would be the line of the roof just around the nearest corner. Pirie moved on, pressing her hands against the shingles with each sideways step. The rain beat down upon her, pressing her blouse tight against her skin and then, suddenly, as she was almost to the corner of the house, her foot, sliding along the drain, fell off into thin air. She fell, twisting her body and grabbing at the wet, slippery shingles and the thunderclap drowned out her half-scream. But she slid off the wet slope and felt herself falling. Blindly, she grabbed out at the air and her hands clasped something metal and she clung to it, wrapping her legs around it and hanging there till she dared to realize she was still alive. She looked around to see she was clinging to the drainpipe at the very corner of the house where it connected to the copper gutter. Peering down, she saw that it disappeared into the darkness below and she dared not try to slide down it. The hall window beckoned only a few feet further at the other side of the house and, using her last bit of strength, Pirie pulled herself back up onto the rain gutter of the roof.

The rain had stopped beating against her so furiously, though it still came down steadily; she moved on trembling legs to the window. This one was easy to reach and she leaned her arms on the sill for a few minutes before pushing it open. Slithering snake-like over the window sill, Pirie eased her body into the house and the blackness of the hallway, crouching silently, listening. But there was no sound and she got up to move down the hall. At her first step she heard the water splash onto the floor from her soaked clothes and she stopped at once. When she reached the stairs, with the old, worn carpeting on them, she would leave a trail of wet spots that would easily last the few hours till morning. And it would lead from the third floor directly to her room, a clear signal for Valonia to scour her room again. She'd be certain to discover the missing bottle.

Turning to the window, Pirie opened it again and peeled off her wet clothes. She squeezed them out over the edge of the window and wrung the major part of the water from them. Then, putting on her shirt and panties, she tried both legs of the jeans in a loose knot around her neck. In the darkness, she hurried to the top of the stairs and paused there. There was still the matter of her wet footprints on the carpet and suddenly she smiled as long ago flashed before her eyes. With one lithe motion, ignoring the sore muscles of her pain-wracked body, she swung her long, slender legs over the smooth bannister and slid down to the bend in the stairs midway between the floors. There she stepped down on tip-toe for a moment and then swung herself over the bannister to slide down the remaining half of the stairway. She had often done it as a little girl. At the second floor landing, she hopped nimbly over the carpet and padded down the wood floor of the hall to her room. There, she threw her wet things into the tub, slipped under the sheets, still clutching the bottle in her hand, and let the soft sound of the rain as it came to a halt put her to sleep.

She woke up once, in the light of dawn, sitting bolt upright in the bed with a vision of herself falling from a rooftop. But she lay down again and quickly found her way back to sleep. When the sun entered her room to make its way across the bed, she woke and let the warm rays penetrate the bruised, aching muscles of her legs. Finally she rose and took a long, hot bath, soaking in the welcome heat of the water, washing the caked blood and grime from numerous small scrapes and cuts on her arms and feet and upper legs. She heard Peely come in while she was still in the bath and called out that she'd be right down. But she waited till she heard Peely go out and then hurried out to don slacks and a long-sleeved shirt. She locked the bottle of medicine in her suitcase and hung the key around her neck on a small gold chain. Downstairs, Peely was waiting breakfast and the two girls ate together.

When they'd finished and Valonia came in to clear away the dishes, Pirie glanced up at the woman's impassive face.

"Did I hear you up last night, Valonia?" she asked, surprised at her own boldness.

"I went up to my room," the woman answered. "I suddenly thought I'd left the window open. The storm woke me."

Valonia walked out of the room and Pirie's eyes narrowed in thought. Was it that simple an explanation? Perhaps, but she couldn't quite bring herself to believe it. And there was irony in that, too. Only a few short days ago she'd been unwilling to believe anything that wasn't clear and rational and now it was the clear and rational she found hard to believe. But the night had passed and she had achieved her objective. She counted the hours till Adam would come by. He would be proud of her, though she'd wait a long time before telling him what she'd gone through. She stayed close to Peely, who seemed very listless and tired and perfectly content to stretch out on the lawn and watch the dragonflies and giant swallowtails fly about.

"I was awake most of the night listening to the storm, you know," Peely remarked offhandedly later in the afternoon and Pirie felt her heart skip a beat.

"You were awake, too, weren't you, Pirie?" Peely added and Pirie's heart stood still.

"No, I wasn't, hon," Pirie said, struggling to keep her voice casual.

"Yes, you were," Peely answered, her voice sing-song.

"What makes you say that, Peely?" Pirie asked, frightened of the answer.

"I just know," was all Peely replied and, closing her eyes fell into a light sleep on the sun-warmed grass. Pirie breathed a sigh of relief and decided against pursuing the subject further. She was glad, terribly glad, to see the sun begin to lower. Later, as Peely went inside to idly play at the piano, she stayed by the front door, waiting for Adam to arrive. But it was Byron Lee's convertible that drove into sight and came to a halt some yards from the house. Byron, resplendent in a maroon blazer and white slacks, waved her out and Pirie walked to the car. She hadn't seen

Byron since the day he'd suggested she visit Doc Asher and he, of course, knew nothing about the bridge incident. Not unless he was guilty—so she put on a pleasant smile for him. His grin, rakish and as full of charm as ever, held her and he took her arm.

"I've just come by for a minute, gorgeous," he said. "I heard about Doctor Gallagher, of course. Tough luck. I know you wanted to see him about Peely."

She nodded and said nothing, deciding to let Byron carry the conversation. His black-brown eyes held hers intently and his dark handsomeness, his animal sensuousness, seemed to reach out to her insistently. She had to be careful, she knew, and not seem cold and distant. After all, their last meeting had been a very nice one and he'd seemed sincerely interested in her welfare and that of Peely. He didn't know she had harbored dark suspicions about him, in fact still harbored them deep down inside her. And so she let him take her by the shoulders and look deeply into her eyes.

"I've come out to tell you to take my advice and sell Moonwater to me," she heard him say and the intenseness of his eyes surprised her.

"I thought we'd exhausted that subject, Byron," Pirie said quietly.

"No," Byron Lee snapped, the charm vanishing from his voice, his dark eyes boring into her. "I'm not through with it. I'm trying to help you, dammit."

"Then I'm appreciative, Byron." Pirie tried not to sound cynical. "But I told you I won't sell, certainly not until Peely's well and able to discuss it intelligently."

"You can't wait for that," Byron said through clenched jaws. "I'm telling you what's best for you. Agree to sell. Get away from here. You don't want the place anyway."

"It's not what I want, Byron," Pirie said and she felt the man's hands on her shoulders digging in, tightening in anger. "You're hurting me, Byron." She watched him gather himself and step back, dropping his hands from her. Was he envisioning them around her throat, she wondered? There was a rage inside him, all right, and his dark, intense handsomeness had turned into something frightening.

"You'll be sorry," he said to her. "Dammit, you'll be sorry you didn't listen to me. Don't tell me I didn't try."

Turning abruptly, he leaped into the car and roared away, disappearing into the dusk. She watched the red glow of his taillights through the leaves and vines until the bayou denseness swallowed them up. She let her breath out in a long sigh and felt her palms grow wet with cold perspiration. There was no question about Byron being a suspect now, she told herself. She had tried to dismiss him but this was a different Byron Lee Hodges from the one she'd once known. This was a man with a raging temper, a man who could kill, a man driven by his own ambitions and objectives. She had seen a ruthlessness in him tonight, the kind of ruthlessness that seizes the frightened and she wondered about that. He had seemed upset to the point of being frightened. Did he wonder if she suspected him and, having had his fears confirmed, explode in sudden alarm? Pirie went to the front door and sat down on the wide step outside it. She would skip dinner. Her stomach was doing cartwheels anyway. It hadn't simmered down yet from the night before.

The dusk had turned to night and the dinner hour was over when she saw the first flashes of headlights along the bayou road from Grandview. She was on her feet, hurrying onto the lawn, when Adam came to a halt and once again she was astonished by the depth and speed of his perceptiveness.

"What's wrong, Pirie?" he asked before she could say a word. "You're upset."

"A little," she admitted. "Byron Lee Hodges stopped by about an hour ago." With one hand on his arm, Pirie quickly told Adam what had taken place and the young lawyer listened without interrupting.

"I guess it shook me up a bit," Pirie said, concluding her story. "I was letting emotions, sentiment, get in the way of judgment by refusing to really believe Byron could have been the one."

"And now you believe he was?" Adam asked quietly, his gaze searching her face.

"I ... I don't know," Pirie answered. "I don't exclude him anymore. He knew I was going to visit Doc Asher. He practically sent me on the trip. And he knew I intended seeing Doctor Gallagher the next day. He could have killed Doc Gallagher. The pen could have rolled to the left side of the paper as you first suggested. It's all possible."

"And what about the other attempts on your life?" Adam asked her. "What about your conviction that Peely's condition has been caused by Robert Barlow and Valonia?"

Pirie ran a hand across her frowning brow, her mind bogging down under Adam's searching questions. "I don't know," she said, her voice breaking. "I don't know what to think anymore."

She felt his arms pulling her to him, holding her tight and she buried her face into his chest, letting the circle of his grasp shut out the world. Finally, she moved back and looked up into Adam's unsmiling face, trying to read the message deep in his eyes. She wasn't sure what she saw there and she was too afraid to hope. But suddenly she felt warm and secure inside.

"I don't blame you for not knowing what to think," Adam said. "I told you, there are strange forces at work here. Did you get that bottle of medicine?"

"Yes," Pirie answered in a happy whisper. "It's in my suitcase. I'll get it right away."

"Good girl," Adam grinned at her. She hurried upstairs, unlocked the suitcase and found the little bottle where she'd hidden it under her still unpacked blouses. Adam would be enraged if he knew how close she'd toyed with death to get it, she knew. It was nice to know someone cared enough to get angry. Slipping the bottle into the pocket of her slacks, she opened the door to see the towering form of Valonia standing there. Fighting off the instinctive desire to flinch back, Pirie held her ground.

"Yes?" she said, putting a courage she didn't really possess into her voice.

"Are you going out for the evening with that Adam Bailey?" Valonia growled the question. "Peely wants to know."

"No, he just stopped by for a visit," Pirie said. "Tell Peely I'll be in to see her in a little while."

She brushed past the woman, feeling the strength of her long, hard arms, and hurried down the stairs, her heart pounding in time to her steps. A few more like that and she would die of sheer fright, she murmured silently. She wondered if the woman's question had really been the truth or something hurriedly made up. Adam was in the car and she crawled in beside him, slipping the bottle into his hands. He dropped it into his jacket pocket and squeezed her shoulder approvingly.

"I'm going to drive directly to Cotile with this now," he said. "I want the lab to get at it first thing in the morning. I've been finding out a lot of very interesting things which I'll go into with you tomorrow evening, about this time. In fact, I'll have a few more questions answered by then."

"You haven't made any comment about Byron's visit tonight," Pirie said.

"That's right," Adam smiled at her. "Right now I'm not excluding anyone nor including anyone."

Pirie smiled up at him. He hadn't answered her oblique question about his own feelings but his air of quiet, calm confidence was better medicine than anything else for her.

"I'll let you get on," she said, opening the door of the car. Adam's hand on her shoulder pulled her back and his lips brushed her cheek, not quite a kiss, yet very much a kiss.

"You be careful till I get back," he said, his face stern but his eyes full of something she knew went beyond simple advice. She nodded and got out of the car and he drove away. Things were looking up, in more ways than one. She turned and saw the huge, ugly house staring down at her malevolently, mockingly, and she shuddered. Someone had once said that evil is not easily put to rest. She went to her room fearing the truth of that thought.

CHAPTER NINE

The following day, she and Peely took a long ride through the winding bayou roads. But only after she left a message with Adam's answering service to that effect. She made certain the ride ended by early afternoon, before the dark shapes of night began to toy with the tangled tendrils and vines. In the afternoon she got a phone call from Byron Lee Hodges and answered it with cold anger.

"I'm surprised you have the nerve to call me, Byron," she said. The man's voice, tight and urgent, told her at once that he hadn't called to try to ingratiate himself with her and she was grateful for that.

"Get smart, Pirie," Byron said. "Get away from there. Sell out. Take Peely and leave. All you have to do is promise to sign the agreement with me."

Pirie frowned into the phone. He seemed to be almost pleading with her. Was he trying to warn her or frighten her? Or perhaps it was a little of both, carefully calculated to serve his own interests.

"I gave you my answer," Pirie said coldly. "Please don't bother me anymore."

"You're a damn fool!" Byron shouted over the phone. "You'll be sorry you didn't listen to me."

She hung up and walked away grim-lipped. He'd used almost the same threat last night. Warnings, pleading and threats. Was he just a desperate man caught up in some web of his own? Maybe. But desperate men do desperate things, an inner voice reminded her. She went into the living room where Peely waited and the two sisters spent the remainder of the day together. At dinner Peely seemed genuinely tired and toyed with her food. Pirie continued to meet Robert Barlow at his own game of false geniality and detested every minute of it. When Adam's cream-colored car pulled up in front of the old house she was outside, waiting for him again, and once more told him of Byron's threats and warnings. They walked to the deep shadows at the edge of the lawn where the willows and acacias and blackgums formed the edge of the tangled bayou land.

"I did some checking on Byron Lee Hodges," Adam began. "He has real money problems and he's been tied in with some shady real estate people with out-of-state capital. He's no doubt desperate to please his associates. He's into them for quite a bit of money."

"Then it's true?" Pirie asked. "Byron is the one?"

"Possibly," was all Adam would say. "But I've a few more eye-openers for you. The lab analysis of that medicine showed it to be made up of crushed Mandrake and cohaba and a few unimportant ingredients. Cohaba is a ritual hallucinatory drug used primarily in the West Indies and Central South America, but sometimes in Europe. It causes temporary madness, excitement, and periods of tranquility but most important, it seems to heighten every mental process involved in awareness. Like most of these drugs, no one really knows what it does to the mind. The Mandrake, of course, contributed its narcotic effects."

"My God!" Pirie whispered. "Then the medicine is responsible for Peely's lethargy and disoriented flights of fancy."

"Undoubtedly," Adam said. "But remember, she did describe that dress, didn't she?"

"Yes," Pirie said. "Which means?"

"That even counting the influence of the drugs, there are things we don't know and can't explain," Adam answered. "Which brings me to that near-fatal accident you had on the way from New York. In the world of the occult, the opal is a stone of evil and can strengthen the powers of the evil person over the wearer. The number nine is a mystically powerful number, the double triad. There are nine orders of angels, nine orders of devils, a nine-fold gate of hell and it was a nine-day period in which Satan and his angels fell from grace and heaven. The opal amulet you wore had nine points, I might add."

Pirie searched Adam's face, her eyes wide with shock. "Surely you don't believe in things like this, do you?" she asked.

"No, I don't believe in them," Adam said. "But that accident happened, didn't it? You told me yourself how you felt the wheel turn into the path of the oncoming car, as though unseen hands were pulling your grip right at it. Call it a concordance of evil, an example of black magic—call it whatever you like, but it happened and I can't write it off as a coincidence."

Pirie felt her hands reaching out to Adam and his arms drew her against him, her head pressed tightly to his shoulder. Suddenly she was trembling and filled with a terrible fear.

"But things like that just don't happen," she tried again.

"Don't they?" Adam said, and the words reverberated inside her with hollow mockery. They did happen and she had seen more than enough examples of the paranormal experiences beyond our understanding.

"Oh, Adam, I'm frightened, really frightened," she whispered. "We can't fight the unknown."

"No, but we can fight the known," he said. "The forces being employed here are being directed by those whom we can fight."

"Valonia and Barlow," she said. "It must be them. She gave me the amulet. They've been giving Peely the medicine. Where does Doc Asher fit into this, Adam?"

"I don't have all the pieces put together yet," Adam said. "And there are a number of pieces. But I'm going to Alexandria to check out a few more items I've been pursuing and when I get back I'll have the answers."

"Yes, there are pieces called Byron Lee Hodges and Doc Asher," Pirie said.

"And others you don't suspect," Adam said. "For instance, haven't you ever thought about the name Valonia? It's a rather unusual name."

"I guess it is," Pirie shrugged. "I just assumed it was a European name of some sort."

"It is that," Adam said grimly. "Valonia is the name of the European or Valonia Oak tree. The acorn cups of the Valonia oak are considered by some sources to contain a magical cure because the Valonia Oak is a sacred tree to the occult world. Ink made from these acorn cups was used for the writing of spells centuries ago."

"Then what is she, Adam?" Pirie asked, feeling her skin crawling. "A sorceress, a witch of some kind? Is Barlow one, too? The whole thing is beyond belief."

"Is it?" Adam asked, his face unsmiling, serious. Once again she knew that it was not beyond belief, only beyond understanding and comprehension.

"I don't know what they are, Pirie," Adam said. "But I've done a lot of homework since you came to me with your story. I've been tracing down bits and pieces. You've been living it and we come out at the same place. There are powers and forces far beyond those of our ordinary existence. But they are there and signs of them are around us more often than we realize, or allow ourselves to realize."

"When will you be back, Adam?" she asked.

"By tomorrow evening," he said quickly. "You can count on it. The only reason I don't take you and Peely away now is because that would let them know something had gone wrong. They can't be permitted to get away. A man has been murdered, to say nothing of the attempts on your life. The guilty ones must be brought to justice."

Pirie lifted her head and suddenly Adam's lips were on hers, strong yet soft, pressing down on her mouth, parting her lips, tasting the sweetness of her. He kissed her hard and long and she wanted only to have him continue, but finally he pulled away, his hands cupping her face between them.

"I've a lot of reasons to hurry back," he said and she knew what he meant. Hand in hand, they walked to the car and Pirie gazed up at the soft moonlight that bathed the lawn.

"It will be a full moon tomorrow night," she said. "Moonwater." She laughed at Adam's little frown of puzzlement. "That's the only time the moon is strong enough to break through to shine on the bayous."

"Ah, now I understand why the house was named Moonwater," he said. "I often wondered what it meant."

He got into the car and drove away with a kiss blown to her from the window. She watched him disappear and then went into the house. She was glad Valonia was in the kitchen, the sound of her clear through the swinging door, and Barlow somewhere out of sight. She didn't want to see them, not yet, not until she'd had the night to digest the things Adam had told her. She looked in on Peely and went over to the girl's sleeping figure. "It'll all be over soon, hon," she whispered. "Once you're off that 'medicine' you'll snap right back to normal."

Pirie tip-toed from the room and went to her own room where, locking the door, she undressed and lay awake in the dark. Adam had told her so much, so many things, that she had to digest them all one by one, and there were still huge gaps. They'd spoken of Valonia and Barlow but they'd never touched on why they wanted to kill her, or why they were bent on giving Peely hallucinatory drugs under the guise of medicine. Maybe that was one of the answers he still had to find. And what of Byron and Doc Asher? Where did they fit in? She toyed with suppositions of her own and found each one wanting. She thought of Adam's lips on hers and felt her body respond at once to the thought. It wasn't mere gratefulness, she knew now. In his eyes she had seen that something else that went beyond excitement as he looked at her, that something so much harder to find.

She thought about Adam as long as she could, and about happier days, and about anything that would keep her mind from the dark forces of Valonia and Barlow. But finally she realized she could not hide from it and she let her mind think about the unknown and felt the cold chill that immediately enveloped her. The terrible thought festering in her mind burst out as she forced herself to face it. Had they made Peely one of them with their drugs and God-knows-what-other strange powers? She had seen the dress without having ever seen it. She had known Pirie was awake the other night without having seen her. And the morning after the murder attempt at the bridge, Peely had been cross and sullen. That very afternoon she had run away, ridden aimlessly for hours. Had she been running from a vision that something terrible was about to happen? She had never asked why Doctor Gallagher hadn't come that fateful afternoon. She was completely calm, with the lack of curiosity of someone who never expected him to show up in the first place. Had they made Peely one of them, she asked herself again? Had they given her black powers that, once given, were forever there? Or was it the drugs alone that gave her flashes of spiritual vision? Would she "snap back to normal" once the drugs were taken away?

Hurry back, Adam, she breathed into the dark. *Hurry back with those answers. There are too many questions haunting the night.*

But sleep finally came to the girl and she greeted the day with a strange feeling of mixed hope and uneasiness. Once more she would spend the day close to Peely, being both protector and protected in the girl's presence. Peely was still combing her hair when Pirie went downstairs to see Barlow and Valonia talking in guarded tones in the kitchen. They broke off at once as Pirie entered and Robert Barlow's smooth, contained arrogance was replaced by something else—a sharp-eyed, cold stare. Pirie felt her own invisible antennae rise at once. Something had gone wrong. Had Valonia discovered the bottle missing? Had word of Adam's discoveries and investigations come to them somehow? Or did they have their own dark ways of knowing that things were running against them? She couldn't know which it was, only that something was wrong. Peely came down and the girls breakfasted together. Pirie, tired of slacks, had put on a leather skirt and a white silk blouse with a wide collar. Peely had been given her morning dose of medicine on waking, it was plain to see, and Pirie's lips set grimly. Valonia came into the room and Pirie saw hatred in the woman's eyes; she returned the glance measure for measure.

"I'd like to go into town," Peely announced.

"Doc Asher doesn't want you going into town," Valonia said. "He wants you to stay quiet here and rest."

"I think it would be good to get into town," Pirie countered, getting to her feet. Valonia moved to the door, her towering frame blocking it, her long arms hanging loosely.

"No," she said. "She doesn't leave here." Pirie saw the movement out of the corner of her eye and glanced over to see Robert Barlow standing in the other doorway, his eyes narrowed, the handsome face sharp and cold. The threat hung in the air, unspoken, invisible, but so terribly real, the reality of that which doesn't tangibly exist. It was no more than appropriate, though. The real was unreal here at Moonwater and the unreal was real. Pirie shrugged and turned away. Yesterday she would have risked meeting the challenge head on. Today she was afraid, very afraid. There was a new, menacing note to Barlow and the woman, perhaps born of desperation. She would back down and wait for the night and Adam.

"Come on, Peely," Pirie said, taking the younger girl's hand. "We'll go for a walk instead."

Valonia moved from the doorway and Pirie thought she read a sense of relief in the towering woman's eyes. As the girls walked across the lawn, Pirie noted that Peely's aimless eyes were never still and a small, secretive smile played around her lips. She caught the quick, sideward glance Peely threw her way.

"It's going to be moonwater tonight," Peely said. "And someone's going to die."

She tossed the remark off with an airy casualness that made it all the more numbing. Pirie stopped in her tracks, pinpoints of ice stabbing into her body like so mant darts being flung at her.

"Don't say things like that, Peely," she exclaimed.

"Why not?" Peely smiled softly. "It's true."

"How do you know it's true?" Pirie asked, her hands closing on Peely's shoulders, almost shaking the girl. "What do you see that makes you say that?"

"I don't see anything." Peely's face tightened in a frown of brief concentration. Then she brightened and looked calmly happy. "I just know it will happen."

"No," Pirie snapped. "No one is going to die. That's nothing but your imagination, Peely." And as she spoke, she wondered whom she was trying most to convince, Peely or herself. But Peely was maddeningly casual in her insistence.

"No, someone will die at moonwater time," she said. "But I'm not afraid. I'm not afraid at all."

As Pirie looked on in growing despair, Peely began to recite in a clear, sing-song voice.

"No evil thing that walks by night,
In fog or fire, by lake or moorish fen,
Blue meagre hag, or stubborn unlaid ghost,
That breaks his magic chains at curfew time,
No goblin, or swart faery of the mine,
Hath hurtful power over true virginity."

"Where did you learn that?" Pirie asked as the other girl stretched idly.

"Valonia taught it to me," Peely answered. "So I wouldn't ever be afraid."

Peely spun away, half skipped in a small circle and lay down on the grass as Pirie sank down beside her.

"I'm tired, Pirie," the girl said. "And I have a headache. I want to rest. Stay here with me while I rest."

Peely closed her eyes and in seconds she was asleep, her breathing shallow, steady. Pirie felt herself trembling inwardly, wondering what it all meant. Why was Peely's not "ever being afraid" so important to Valonia? Why had she cloaked Peely's drugged, disoriented mind with the armor of bravery? It was unfathomable, like just about everything else concerning the woman. Pirie heard the girl's words revolving around her mind— chilling, terrifying, offering no clue for interpretation. "Someone will die at moonwater time, but I'm not afraid."

All Pirie could think of was to rush to the phone, to call Adam, but he was in Alexandria. There was nothing to do but wait till he returned. Wait and wrestle with a thousand fearful thoughts. Pirie looked down at Peely and wondered if the girl's remark had been little more than the result of disoriented imaginings. Because Peely had been able to see in strange ways, through the inner senses of the mind's eye, did not make her infallible. The drugs in the medicine created disturbed pictures of the soul; hallucinations, strange visions. Perhaps this was mere distortion and no more than that. But Pirie felt herself swallow with difficulty, her throat dry, tight, as her mind raced on. What if Peely was seeing once again with her inner senses? What if this was a crystal clear premonition of the future? Who would be killed this night, she asked herself and her answer swam out of her subconscious in the form of another question. Whom had death doggedly pursued? Pirie shut her eyes tightly and prayed for Adam to hurry back.

Later, when Peely woke, the two girls went into the house, into the library, got out old volumes from their childhood and the afternoon soon passed to dusk. There had been two phone calls, both for Robert Barlow and taken in the study in low, guarded tones. Valonia stayed in the kitchen or went back and forth to her room, her heavy footsteps echoing in the stillness of the house. She fixed dinner but only Peely ate on a small tray. Pirie had no stomach for food and, gazing out at the gathering dusk, she wished she could push back the coming night. With every new shadow, she felt herself grow more tense, until her fists were clenched and stiff. Darkness had come and Peely, tired, had gone to her room, leaving Pirie alone in the library. A stillness had come over the house, broken only by the sound of Valonia's footsteps upstairs as she moved about. Pirie stayed by the window, perched on the narrow, leather-covered window seat, and peered out into the night, trying to hurry Adam to her by the force of her thoughts. Soon the moon would rise high in the sky and bathe the bayous in its cold light.

The phone, when it rang, startled her so that she jumped into the air. She ran to it, taking up the receiver with trembling hands.

"Pirie? It's me, Adam," the voice said, very faint and muffled and distant.

"Oh, Adam, where are you?" Pirie cried out. "I can hardly hear you."

"Bad connection," he said. "I've been delayed." His voice, strained and muffled, faded away entirely.

"I can't hear you, Adam," Pirie shouted into the phone, fearful anxiety in her voice.

"Go to Doc Asher's place," the voice said, coming back just strong enough to hear, barely audible. "Meet me there. I'll explain then."

"What about Peely?" Pirie exclaimed.

"All right," the voice sounded over the line, hollow and muffled. "She'll be all right. Get going."

"Adam. ..." Pirie called but the line was dead, silent, and she put the phone down with dread and confusion inside her. But she would have to go. Adam wouldn't have her meet him there without good reason, she knew. No doubt he'd uncovered something important about the backwoods medicine man. Perhaps he needed her there to witness a confession he intended to extract from the man. Or, and Pirie paused, perhaps he'd found that Asher was the key figure in all that had happened. She hadn't given that possibility any thought at all. Hurrying, Pirie looked in on Peely, saw the girl was asleep on her bed, and left quietly.

Thomas was still at the stables and once again he hitched the buckboard up for her, a frown of unvoiced curiosity on his face. Gathering her courage, she drove off into the back roads of the bayou land and was immediately enveloped in the blackness. The moon hadn't yet risen high enough to pierce the fierce denseness. But it would, she knew, and then the bayous would be an even more unearthly place for, on the moonwater nights, every creeping, crawling, hunting creature of land and water was drawn to the silver ribbons of water. It was known by every trapper, every bayou man, that on moonwater nights the bayous came alive as at no other time, drawn by the same strange force that controls the ocean tides. The force of the moon, Pirie thought grimly, one more force which eluded man's understanding. She drove the buckboard fast, recklessly, anxious to be out of this hanging, clutching place, and she halted only when she came to the little bridge across Thompson's marsh. There she hopped from the buckboard and carefully tested each wide plank with her foot before driving across the bridge. On the other side she spurred the horse on, ducking low in the seat to avoid the grasping vines and aerial roots. She saw the faint yellow glow ahead, the lights from Doc Asher's house, and she wheeled the buckboard into the yard quietly, slowing the horse before reaching the small clearing. She stepped down and waited for a moment, scanning the silent house, a small oasis of light in the surrounding blackness. The front door was open but there was no one to be seen moving about inside, and she was certain Adam hadn't arrived yet. In fact, she found herself suddenly wondering just how he would arrive. Moving on the balls of her feet, she crossed the few steps to the house and peered into the nearest window. On the floor lay a large rag doll, crumpled, with the long handle of a very long kitchen knife sticking up from between its shoulder blades. Only it wasn't a rag doll, she saw as she stared at it in mounting horror. It was Doc Asher. She stood gazing in through the window, transfixed at the sight; so brutally unreal, so terrifyingly real. The movement inside the room made her tear her eyes away from the murdered man and she saw a figure emerging from an adjoining room, tall, intense with a reckless handsomeness and she felt her lips soundlessly form the name *Byron*. She saw Byron Lee Hodges step over the slain figure and move toward the door, and suddenly she realized he'd be outside in a moment and see her standing there.

Whirling, she turned to flee and her foot came down on a small round stone, just large enough to turn her ankle. She felt herself fall, heard her sharp, involuntary cry of pain and then she was on the ground, looking up at Byron standing in the doorway of the little house. It had all happened so fast—but it was clear now, spelled out in deed, and her eyes held their accusation. Byron had been the one all along and now, for reasons yet unclear, he had had to kill Doc Asher. Pirie pulled herself to her feet, the act breaking the spell of the moment when Byron had stood frozen in the doorway and she lay motionless on the ground.

"Stop!" Byron yelled as Pirie ran for the buckboard. She had reached it and was half way onto the seat when she felt his hands seize her, dragging her from the wagon. Terror lending her strength, she kicked out and felt her shoe hit hard against his leg. He gasped in pain and she tore from his grasp, clawing out, raking his face with her fingernails.

"Murderer," she screamed in fury. She turned to run but he was upon her at once, this time flinging her to the ground.

"No, damn you," she heard him mutter. "You're not pinning a murder rap on me."

His arm came down across her throat and she felt her breath shut off at once. Twisting her body, she got a knee up and kicked out, sinking her foot deep into Byron Lee's groin. He groaned in pain and the pressure of his arm on her throat let up. Casting out with her elbow she heard the satisfying sound of it hitting his nose and she rolled away, twisting and clawing and fighting for her life. Leaping to her feet she tried for the buckboard again but Byron, his face contorted with rage, catapulted forward to seize the reins. He missed and fell forward and the horse reared up in fright, pawed the air and came down galloping. Pirie went flying across the ground as the rear wheel of the buckboard slammed into her shoulder. She landed at the edge of the blackness and saw Byron getting to his feet, starting for her.

She flung herself backwards, into the blackness of the dense hanging vines and monstrous Mangrove trunks. She dove behind a broad trunk and lay still, hearing Byron move into the blackness, his breath harsh. She heard him move off to the right and she shifted her body to the other side of the trunk. He was still too close to run for it. If she could get to the other side of the clearing, where the bayou ran close to the house, she could slip into the water. She lay still, holding her breath as she listened to the man's figure moving back toward her. He moved slowly, taking the time to search each tangle of roots and circle each trunk. She heard him curse as he stumbled and fell and then got up again. She took the moment to crawl closer to the edge of the clearing. She'd make a run for it if he went just a little deeper into the tangle roots and ferns. She moved again, pressing her hands down on the soft shoestring fern to pull herself forward silently. But under her hand a small green snake twisted itself in fright and slithered away. Involuntarily, Pirie heard the small gasp of fright escape her. It was more than enough. She heard Byron Lee rushing toward her and she rose to run. But he was fast, his hand seizing her by the hair, his other arm coming around her neck. And then she heard her name being called.

"Pirie," the voice called to her. "Pirie, are you here?"

"Adam!" the girl screamed and in the small clearing by the house she saw Adam's figure, halted at the doorway. He spun around as her scream resounded and she felt herself flung away, felt herself falling face down and Byron's form racing past her to the clearing. She caught a glimpse of a length of wood in his hand as he charged out of the foliage into the light.

"Adam, look out!" she screamed again and swallowed a mouthful of dirt. When she got to her feet and stumbled into the clearing Byron Lee was circling Adam, swinging viciously with the thick length of wood in his hand. Adam moved backwards, in a crouch, trying to avoid the frenzied lunges of his adversary. He feinted, going to his left and Byron swung hard, but Adam came up under the swing and Pirie saw his blow, fast and hard, land alongside Byron's jaw. Byron staggered back and Adam struck again, a left this time, to the point of the taller man's jaw. Byron dropped to his knees, rolled over, the club falling from his hands. Adam kicked it aside and moved toward the other man. Byron lunged forward but Adam, moving with cat-like grace, avoided the lunge and sent the other man sprawling across the ground with a half-blow, half-shove. Byron, bleeding from his mouth now as well as from the scratches Pirie had raked across his face, rolled over and came up running, dashing for the darkness of the bayous.

"He's getting away," Pirie exclaimed, rushing forward into Adam's arms.

"Let him," Adam said quietly.

"But he killed Doc Asher," Pirie exclaimed. "He's the one behind it all."

"No, not really," Adam said quietly, holding her trembling body close. "Byron was involved, but only at the edges."

"Then why did he try to kill me just now?" Pirie demanded.

"Fear and desperation," Adam said. "He just came apart at the seams. Your seeing him here could sustain a murder charge and a possible conviction on circumstantial evidence. He knew that and he snapped."

"Then who killed Doc Asher?"

"The same person who told you to come out here," Adam said. Pirie's eyes darkened. "You told me to come here," she said quietly.

"That wasn't me on the phone," Adam answered. "Though, as luck would have it, I was delayed getting back. But I tried getting through to you all afternoon and your phone was apparently out of order, according to the operator. I suspected something had gone wrong and I went straight to Moonwater where Thomas told me you'd gone with the buckboard. I knew there was only one place you'd need the buckboard to get to and I asked Thomas for the rig. He told me I could make better time, more direct, on the bayous. He helped me get one of the pirogues you keep behind the stables down to the water."

Pirie nodded. Her father had always kept two or three of the narrow, shallow-draft boats used by all the bayou people.

"Then it was Barlow who called and told me to come here," she said. "And Barlow killed Doc Asher."

"Yes," Adam nodded. "Not that anyone could prove that from a knife no doubt wiped clean of all fingerprints. Any passing thief could have done it."

Suddenly, as Pirie stared at Adam, the terrible, shattering thought burst upon her with the fiery fury of a bolt from hell.

"*Peely!*" she shouted. "Peely's going to die. We've got to get back there."

Now it was Adam's turn to frown. "They won't do anything to Peely now," he said. "That would be too obvious. They've been too clever all along to make that blunder now."

"They've already done it," Pirie heard herself shout. "Peely isn't afraid. It's moonwater and she'll die. It's what they've been preparing for."

She was clutching at Adam, pulling him along and she saw his eyes, narrowed, following the disjointed pattern of what she'd said. Then he exploded in anger.

"Of course!" he said through clenched teeth. "That's it, the part I hadn't yet figured out." He raced off ahead of her, running toward the spot where he'd left the pirogue.

"Dammit, dammit, dammit!" She heard him saying. "It's so clear now. I should have seen it. I should have seen it."

Nothing was that clear to Pirie, except the part about Peely and death at moonwater time. Dark and powerful forces had been given to Peely, forces that would lead her without fear to seek out the terrors of the night and there to die. Perhaps, and the thought was suffocating, it was already too late. Adam had the pirogue in the water already and she clambered in, holding onto the sides of the narrow little craft. Adam paddled out into the bayou with long, powerful strokes. "I'll tell you what I learned as we go," he said. "You know these bayous better than I do. Make sure I don't take any wrong turns."

Pirie nodded and her heart sank as she saw the moonlight begin to paint the water with its blue-white, ghostly brush.

CHAPTER TEN

The old house stood wrapped in silence and darkness. Outside, the moon rose high and full and bathed the bayous with its light that was more than light, light that was a silvered force, a caliginous power, an unearthly magnet. The creatures of the night stirred and emerged from the dark. From every secret hiding place they came, from burrows and logs, from nests and brush, caves and earthen holes. They came to the silver water licking the mossy banks, beckoning silently.

They came, by ones and by twos, crawling, sliding, swimming. They came to the call of the moon, the voice of the cold light, the cry of the night turned blue-ghost silver. They came in answer to a silent signal, a tropism of a world neither known nor understood.

And as the eaves and gables of the silent old house were touched by the silvered light, the girl sat up in the blackness of the room and moved to the window. Lips half parted in quiet excitement, she stood looking out at the softly glowing light and then, her filmy nightgown trailing behind her, she went down the stairs and out into the night. Moving like a wraith, the moonglow turning her blond hair into silver, she walked on bare feet across the dew-misted grass, into the dense tangled aerial roots. Her eyes burned with a new brightness as they searched the vines and Mangroves, the cypresses and willows, and she glimpsed the blue-white ribbon of the bayous ahead and quickened her pace.

A white-eared fox-squirrel fled from her path and a 'possum halted, bared its teeth and moved away. A big indigo snake, black hide shining in the moonlight, slipped away, but a giant Diamond-backed rattlesnake coiled and held its ground. Fire flies and bullfrogs, giant luna moths and night beetles, all swarmed and croaked and swooped around the thin figure that moved through their domain. In the silver ribbon, a big 'gator floated unmoving in the slow current, a silver-touched log. The barefoot form sang softly to herself as she passed through grasping, clutching vines.

"No evil thing that walks by night, in fog or fire, by lake or moorish fen. ...." the girl's voice sounded in the lighted dark and when she reached the bank, the nut moss a dark green carpet under her feet, she halted. She stared at the bayou, usually so darkly ominous, now so beautifully shining, beckoning. A small frown creased her brow and she seemed to draw back, suddenly caught in an inner struggle. A moment's fright leaped into her face—but then she looked upwards at the blue-white sphere in the heavens, and she smiled. In the night, the eyes of a thousand creatures watched her, most of them only curious observers. But not all. There were those who watched from back in the Mangrove thickets, watched and held their breaths.

Finally, the girl stepped into the water, letting the warm wetness billow up under her nightgown, moving deeper until she struck out, letting the slow current carry her away from the bank. Her nightgown ballooned around her until she resembled a giant water lily pad with a center of long, blond hair. She let herself float easily on the surface and from the far bank a big copperhead slipped into the water to investigate this huge lily pad. The big 'gator, only the top of his ribbed back, bulbous eyes and long snout above water, blinked as the strange object floated toward him.

The girl was unafraid of the night and she put her head back in the warm water, reveling in the softness of it, her eyes half closed. She could float effortlessly and she did so, unmindful of the deadly dangers that surrounded her, unmindful and unafraid and very close to death.

The pirogue cut through the bayou water propelled by the powerful strokes of Adam's paddle. Pirie searched the winding path of the estuary, looking for familiar shapes and forms. She knew they were getting closer to Moonwater but there was still a long way to go and with every passing moment, as the moonwater of the bayou glinted more invitingly, her heart sank. Between strokes, Adam had started to tell her what he had found out, first in the County Courthouse where an examination of the marriage license of Missy and Robert Barlow showed that Barlow entered America from Serbia on May 10th, 1959.

"Through contacts in the Immigration Department I had all entries for that date checked out," Adam went on. "I found that a Robert Barloch had entered America from Serbia on that date. And in the Grandview County land records I found that a man named Mikhail Barloch bought land in Grandview County in 1802."

"That's over a hundred and fifty years ago," Pirie exclaimed.

"This Mikhail Barloch was undoubtedly the man who originally built Moonwater," Adam said. "Through my same contact, I had him get in touch with some experts in ancient Middle European history. It became apparent that Barlow, really Barloch, had come here to reclaim Moonwater."

"But why?" Pirie asked. "And is that reason enough to kill and practice all kinds of weird things?"

"That's exactly the reason," Adam said. "In eighteenth century Serbia, I learned, the Barloch clan were notorious dealers in spiritualism and sorcery. Black magic, witchcraft, every facet of the occult world—you name it and the Barlochs dealt in it. According to the beliefs of the occult world, or their part of it anyways, the house built by the original Barloch and in which he died, was a spiritual dwelling place of extreme importance to them and had to be reclaimed by them. Barlow, with Valonia's aid, set out to do just that. When your mother died without transferring Moonwater to him, he had to get rid of Peely."

"Without arousing suspicions of murder, of course," Pirie said grimly. The pieces were falling into place with agonizing speed. The potions to unhinge Peely's mind, the hypocritical concern for her condition, the obvious arrangement with Doc Asher—it was all aimed at one thing, one moment, and that moment was now!

"Oh, Adam, they'll win," Pirie choked out. "They've been conditioning Peely's mind, with drugs and whatever terrible powers they possess; they've been preparing her for moonwater."

"Yes, I know that now. I'd not put that piece in place yet," Adam said. "If Peely drowns or is killed in the bayous they'll be completely above suspicion. There's more, but it'll have to wait till later. You start calling Peely. We must be almost there. If your voice can snap her into reality we might still be in time."

"Peeely!" Pirie shouted at once, screaming the name at the top of her lungs. *"Peeeely!"* she screamed again, knowing she had to pierce the girl's inner spell, that false armor of invincibility they had taken so much time to cloak her with so she would willingly walk into death. She called out again, screaming the cry, and heard the sound of her voice echo through the canals of silver, cascading off the huge cypresses.

The alligator moving toward the giant water lily which was floating directly at him swished his tail and back-watered as the strange scream reverberated through the bayou. Bull frogs fell silent and the furred creatures froze in alarm. Only the big copperhead continued to move lazily through the water. In the center of the billowing lily pad the blond head lifted and listened and frowned. Again the call was heard, screamed through the dark, and it pierced her mind, smashing the strange serenity there, shattering the peace into jagged daggers of reality. The girl glanced around at her surroundings, her eyes widening at the gleaming water, the gnarled vines hanging over her head. She saw the big 'gator move in a circle around her and she screeched in terror.

"There," Pirie shouted to Adam, seeing the white form of the billowed nightgown on the surface of the water.

"We're here, Peely," Adam shouted. "Over here." He paddled the pirogue toward the girl who began to swim to meet them, heading for the bank at the same time. Adam reached down and grabbed Peely's arm as the boat came alongside her and the girl stared at him with wide, uncomprehending eyes. Another stroke put them nose into the bank and Pirie leaped out of the craft to embrace her sister. In the dark Mangrove thicket the two crouching figures rose. The man moved toward the water. The woman turned and headed back to the house. There was no need for words. Each knew what had to be done.

Adam had just pulled the pirogue onto the bank and he was kneeling down beside the soaked, frightened figure of the girl when the dark shadow charged out of the tangled vines, crashing into him from the back and sending the young lawyer falling into the bayou. Pirie screamed as she saw Robert Barlow's silver-gray hair, wild and unkempt, his arrogant face a mask of hatred, and his arms close around Adam's throat. She saw both men disappear for a moment beneath the surface of the water and when they reappeared, Barlow still had his death grip on Adam's throat. Pirie stood transfixed in horror as she saw Adam seem to fall backwards. She was casting about for a stick, a stone, anything to use to help fight Barlow, when she saw Adam's leg come up behind the other man and in seconds Barlow had toppled backwards. Adam lashed out at the man, catching him with a blow to the cheek that sent Barlow falling backwards and under the water's surface. Adam started for him again when Barlow came up, sputtering and coughing, and turned and ran into the bayou, diving forward. As Adam and Pirie watched in spellbound horror, Robert Barlow's body stiffened and his face contorted in pain and Adam saw the fangs of the big copperhead sunk deeply into the man's leg. Barlow screamed and whirled in desperate fury and flung the big snake free. But the quick-acting poison had already entered his bloodstream and she saw Barlow grabbing at his leg. He ran limping, waist high in the water, attempting to swim, disappeared from view and then reappeared, clutching his side.

He tried to run parallel to the bank, stumbled, fell and gasped in pain. He sank beneath the water and Pirie saw his arms emerge, flailing helplessly in the air for a brief moment, until they, too, vanished and the bayou flowed on undisturbed.

Adam lay on the bank beside Pirie and Peely, gathering his strength for a moment.

"What happened, Pirie?" the younger girl questioned. "Why am I here? I don't understand."

"You're all right, hon," Pirie replied. "It's all over at last." She turned to Adam, her eyes questioning, uncertain. "It is over, isn't it, Adam?" she breathed with quiet fervency.

Adam nodded, but before he could speak Pirie turned, seeing the orange glow lighting the night sky. Adam leaped to his feet, pulling her with him and with Peely hurrying along behind, they rushed toward the glow. The sharp, frightening crackle of fire filled the night and the soft glow became an inferno of leaping, raging red-yellow flames as they broke from the denseness onto the lawn. Moonwater stood outlined in the blaze that danced along its sides and leaped from its windows, garlanding each "beautifully ugly" line of it with a ribbon of red.

"Look! There, Adam!" Pirie gasped, pointing to one of the top windows where Valonia's gaunt form stood, framed by the square of fire behind her. She stayed but a moment and then disappeared in a wave of flame and smoke and Pirie thought she heard a scream. She wasn't certain because the flames were crying out with a scream of their own as they consumed the house with an avenging fury. She felt Adam's arm creep around her waist and she leaned against him.

"They have reclaimed Moonwater," he said. "Fire was the only way left for them."

Pirie looked up as Adam's eyes met hers. "Their original plan was that with Peely dead through a tragic 'accident' in the bayous, you would transfer or sell the house to Barlow. He knew you had no desire to retain Moonwater. But when Peely somehow got that letter through to you, and you came back, all their forces had to be brought to work against you. You couldn't be allowed to discover what they'd been doing to Peely."

"With Doc Asher's help," Pirie murmured. "Where did he fit in?"

"Barlow had convinced the old fool that Peely would be an ideal subject for testing the various herb medicines they had compounded," Adam said. "Only Barlow and Valonia really knew the potent properties of the drugs they were using. Asher, always fascinated with the subject of hallucinatory drugs, went along with them. Naturally, he had to be eliminated in time."

"And Byron Lee Hodges?" Pirie asked.

"He actually had a client for Moonwater but Barlow convinced him that if he could get you to agree to sell the place, they would pay him double for it." Adam replied. "Only after you returned did Byron begin to suspect that perhaps Barlow and Valonia were behind Peely's illness. But he was torn between his desperate need for cash and his suspicions."

"So he tried threats and warnings to scare me into selling," Pirie added.

"He had gone to Asher's place tonight to confirm his own worst suspicions," Adam said. "He confided that to one of his real estate associates, I learned. But of course he found Asher dead, and then you came along to place him at the scene and he blew up in fear."

Moonwater was hardly visible now, engulfed in a towering pillar of flame, and Pirie felt her hand tighten around Adam's and even in the heat of the flames a chill swept through her.

"But all those unexplained things, Adam," she said. "Those things Peely saw so correctly, that accident I had on the way here?"

"They will stay unexplained, Pirie," Adam answered, his eyes holding hers, his voice grave. "The 'medicine' helped put Peely into another world where she found forces and powers we do not understand. Without constant doses of the 'medicine' the effects will wear off in about a week and she'll be perfectly all right. She probably won't even remember much of what has happened."

"But it did happen," Pirie said. "All of it, the parts that can be explained and the parts that can't."

"Yes," Adam nodded solemnly. "All of it happened." He turned to Pirie, his arms tightening around her, and suddenly her lips were opened to his, eagerly. Finally he pulled away and cupped his hands around her face.

"Let's go, Pirie," he said. "My car's just at the edge of the lawn. You and Peely can stay at my place and be my guests for a while. In fact, I've been meaning to talk to you about that."

"About being your guest?" Pirie questioned.

"Yes, for a long time," Adam said. "Permanently."

"I think I'd like that," Pirie said, pressing close to him. "I think I knew that on the first day I came back, when I met you in town that afternoon."

"How'd you know that then?" Adam asked.

"I don't know," Pirie shrugged. "A sixth sense, I guess."

She saw Adam's eyes twinkle and she laughed with him. It felt good to laugh again, to really laugh. His arms circled her shoulders and Peely's and they walked to the car. Behind her, the fire was burning out and the old house was no more than burned logs now. But she had glimpsed the unknown, and the world would never be quite the same. Especially on moonwater nights.